A
Harlequin
Romance

1492

THE DRUMMER AND THE SONG

by

JOYCE DINGWELL

HARLEQUIN BOOKS

Winnipeg • Canada   New York • New York

THE DRUMMER AND THE SONG

First published in 1969 by Mills & Boon Limited,
17-19 Foley Street, London, England.

Harlequin Canadian edition published May, 1971
Harlequin U.S. edition published August, 1971

Standard Book Number: 373-51492-1.

Printed in Canada

CHAPTER ONE

OUTSIDE the neat buildings of the Kinrow Stud, where today the last-ever of her uncle's blood sales in Britain was nearing its conclusion, the customary sweet country sounds came raucously punctuated by loud bid and auctioneer's hammer. Peta Milford, gazing out to wide pastures, pollen-golden now it was the verge of English summer, stifled another of the sighs she had resolved, for Uncle Claud's sake, strictly not to permit.

She loved this stable belt of England, loved the studs turning out their sires and brood mares in terrain suitable to their elegant breeding ... soft green grass, crisp air, gentle rain.

It was not her own ground, she had come from Cornwall, but as well as her aunt's and uncle's arms being outstretched after her parents' tragedy it seemed that this countryside had opened up as well. Within a month she had known the first benison of healing.

In the way it often is with relatives living counties apart she had not seen Uncle Claud since she was a small girl, and Aunt Alice was new to her. But in an hour ... less ... she had known she was home in her heart with them.

Mr. Gillett, her solicitor, had suggested that she offer to take over Uncle's clerical work in part repayment ... with a stud like Kinrow there should be plenty of that ... but Uncle Claud had just crinkled his bramble-brown eyes and said, 'Pen-pushing for a Milford? No, I don't think so, Peta, not while there's horses around, eh?'

'Claud,' Aunt Alice had intercepted tactfully, 'Peta mightn't care about horses like you do. She mightn't even ride.'

'A Milford not ride?'

'Thank you, Aunt Alice,' Peta had appreciated, 'but I do care and I do ride . . . in fact it would be unthinkable not riding, but it's still not for me to say.'

'If that's an indication for Uncle to issue an order, I'll oblige,' Uncle Claud had laughed. 'Write her up on our pay sheet, Alice, as Peta Milford: Stablehand.'

'Oh, Uncle, you mean it?'

'I couldn't mean anything else. Now come down and make friends with the boys and girls.'

The 'boys and girls' had been the sires and brood mares, for Kinrow had little staff considering its stock, just Uncle Claud, an outside accountant directing Aunt Alice with the books, old Joe, young Harry, and now Peta.

She had been shown Kinrow's bluest of blue blood in black, bay, brown, chestnut and grey horses. Big horses, small horses, all with orbits of merits and lines of ancestors that made you feel, laughed Uncle, a regular guttersnipe.

Though it was Fancy, with neither orbit nor long line, that Uncle loved the best and had passed on to Peta.

'He's yours, girl. Nothing flash, I just bought him because I liked him. For a horse man that's reason enough.' He had patted the grey.

'I love him already.' Peta had fondled the wide brow above the steady eyes. 'Can I try him out?'

'He's yours, do what you like.'

He had not expected her to take him at his word so quickly, but Peta, not waiting for a saddle, had kicked off her shoes and scrambled up.

'Peter should be the name,' Uncle had chuckled after her, but he had been pleased, for to ride bareback you had to know how to grip.

Peta had just cantered round the meadow and come back to Uncle Claud. There had been tears of gratitude in her goldenish Milford eyes, and Uncle had ruffled her dark honey hair and said, 'There! I knew you'd click.'

'Everything's clicked. After the – fire, I – well, I think I died as well. But now, Uncle, *now*—'

Arms around each other, they had gone up for tea.

It had been an idyllic twelve months that had followed. Kinrow was under sentence ... a highway was scheduled to cut it in two, a housing project to spring up.

But, as Uncle Claud breezed every time the subject came

up, he had been warned about this every year since he had bred his first foal. He'd meet it when it came ... if it came. He had smiled cheerfully at his wife and niece, but Aunt Alice ... Peta remembered achingly now ... had said gently, 'Everything comes, Claud dear. Everything comes.'

They had understood several months later. Aunt Alice had died of something she must have known at that time was hopeless. Uncle Claud had been heartbroken. The news that Kinrow really had to go at last had scarcely touched him. Only Peta had grieved.

She was determined to go with him, though, wherever he went. When he told her it would be Australia, she had been unsurprised. Aunt Alice had been Australian. It was only natural that it would be his choice.

'Actually, Peta, Australia's not the world's best breeding country,' he had shrugged. 'That best would mean a marriage of the soft rains of Ireland and the limestone of Kentucky. New Zealand would have some of both and fit the bill better than Australia. But if I have to get away, as I do have to, and if it has to be right away, as I feel I want it, then it has to be Alice's place. All right with you, girl?'

'Yes, Uncle, of course.'

'This place I've practically settled on is in Tasmania, much further south and much cooler climate. I intend to take several sires and mares and start from there.'

'Yes, Uncle.' From where she sat Peta had looked sadly out on Fancy, cropping under a tree.

'And, of course,' Uncle had nodded, 'himself.'

'Him? You don't mean – You can't mean – I mean, Fancy isn't necessary. I mean—'

'Since when is an old friend unnecessary?' Uncle had pointed out. 'I love him like you do. Where we go, he goes. In fact, he ... and Omar and Brilliant Bess ... go this month.' He paused, then added: 'With their strapper, Peta Milford.'

'And you, Uncle?'

'I'll wind up the affairs here, fly out later to open up with you. I've a lot to do, as you can imagine, but by the time you get out by ship, settle our first lot for their period of quarantine, come back for the second consignment and repeat the process, I should be through.' Again Uncle Claud said, 'All right with you?'

And again, Peta remembered now, plucking a piece of meadowsweet and chewing on it, she had assured him, 'Of course.'

But Mr. Gillett, her solicitor, had been frankly dismayed.

'Australia, yes, Peta.' – He had been an intimate friend of her dead parents. – 'But not where you're going.'

'What's wrong with Tasmania?'

'Nothing. That's the trouble.'

'What do you mean, Mr. Gillett?'

'I was there myself some years ago. The little island is totally unlike the big tough north. It's – well, it's England again. And not just England but the part of England from where you sprang.'

'Cornwall?'

'Yes, Peta. You'll open up old wounds, child. You'll suffer it all twice.'

'Uncle reasons that it's more suited for breeding than the north.' Peta's lips had been held firm to stop a trembling. 'It has to be Australia because of Aunt Alice, in which case it will be best for Kinrow to go down there.'

'For Kinrow, yes. For your uncle, yes. But *you*, Peta?'

Peta had crossed to Mr. Gillett's office window. Nothing much to see except more office windows, but even if there had been she would still have seen the house where the three of them, her parents and herself, had lived before the tragedy, that house, modestly pretty and every inch a home prior to the fire. They had been there at the time. She hadn't. She was here now. They weren't. It was as simple . . . and as heartrending . . . as that.

In the year at Kinrow, in different English countryside, she had more or less recovered. But how would she feel if the background was, as Mr. Gillett insisted, so similar to her childhood and girlhood home?

She had stood a long moment, knuckles whitened as she clenched her hands. Then she had come back to the desk in tight resolution.

'I've turned a page, Mr. Gillett. I'm going out there. In fact I leave as soon as the sales are over, I'll be "maiding" several sires and mares in several journeys. Including' – fondly – 'Fancy, of course.'

'Then if you say so, Peta.' Mr. Gillett had seen her to the door.

The opening day of the sale had been successful, and Uncle Claud had been confident the following days would follow suit. After all, the Kinrow line was a good one, and a buyer would always pay for the best.

'Not always,' Peta had teased. 'You once told me "If you like a horse buy it." That's how a certain astute horse-breeder I know bought our Fancy.'

'Well, isn't Fancy the best?' Uncle had demanded.

'The very best. – Uncle Claud, I don't feel I'm pulling my weight these last days. I've nothing to do. Can't you find me something?'

'The auctioneers have taken over. You and I are only spectators now. But there is something, Peta. You can keep your eye on the stables. Most of the bidders are ones I know, but not all. Every buyer has the same viewing opportunity, and rightly so, but yesterday I noticed a snooper where the public isn't allowed. If you see him, girl—'

'Help him on his way,' nodded Peta. 'I'll do that, Uncle Claud.'

That was what she had intended to do now, watch for interlopers, not dream over pollen-golden meadows … dreaming was a fault in Peta, and rather sheepishly she admitted it … but as usual the beauty of Kinrow had captured her.

'Another bid, Mr. Petterson?' Abstractedly she heard the auctioneer cajoling, and wondered rather disinterestedly where the fabulous Mr. Trentham was, for each day it had been: 'Yes, Mr. Trentham? … Knocked down to Mr. Trentham … One more, Mr. Trentham?' Then later at dinner her uncle's satisfied: 'An excellent day – thanks to Trentham.' By the way he had been buying this Trentham must be a millionaire.

9

She shrugged and turned back from the pastures ... and saw the man. He was standing inside Fancy's stable, which meant as buyer he must be a poor judge, for Fancy was strictly for love alone.

And he wouldn't be a buyer. Not back here. This was the type Uncle Claud had complained about. Behind-the-scenes characters, snoopers, totes, wanting more than the bona fide customers had to be satisfied with, sneaking an extra view. Probably he was spying for someone else.

Angrily Peta went forward, her golden eyes tawny with indignation.

He was a mountain of a man, and had she pre-thought she would have realized that it would be even easier for that camel to go through the eye of a needle than a person of this size to sneak-view. That sort of caper meant jockey height with build to match.

But Peta did not pre-think. She called ringingly ... and life as a strapper had taught her to use her voice so that it carried:

'All right, mister, on your way!'

He didn't turn at once. First, he straightened his back and became ... disconcertingly for Peta ... taller still. Then he slowly pivoted round.

Her first impression was hard-faced, though in all fairness she should have allowed for the sun in his eyes, narrowing them to estimating slits. For the rest he was lean and muscular and rather whipcordish, if that could describe her impression of coiled strength.

He looked down from his six-foot and more on her ... looked deliberately and long.

Now she knew she had made a mistake, but stubbornly, even more than that foolishly, and there is nothing worse than feeling foolish, she held her ground.

'Private property,' she said. 'Out! On your way.'

'Who says?'

'I do.'

'Who else?'

'*I* say so, mister. And what I say in this area of Kinrow goes.'

'Goes where?'

He was preparing to smoke now, doing it in a way you seldom if ever saw around here. He was rolling the tobacco and spreading it on thin paper. It rather puzzled her. His accent she had put down as American. There was that final roll of the 'r' in 'where'. A suggestion of a drawl. But did Americans, quick movers, pause to roll their cigarettes? Westerners, perhaps. Texans. His hat was a little wider in the brim than usual, but by no means a ten-gallon. So what was he?

'Well, had a good look?'

American. That 'well' had been almost 'wa-all'.

'All the look I need. And you've had yours.'

There was an excited stir from the enclosure. Clearly the auctioneer's voice resounded importantly: 'And now, gentlemen, we come to today's climax, we offer Santa Rosa, a superb brown colt by—'

'Excuse me, please.'

The big man was pushing past Peta, and it was a push, for he could have filled the entire door by himself.

It irritated Peta that he was getting off so lightly. Indubitably he was not what Uncle Claud had warned her of, but indubitably, too, he was out of his correct position.

'Don't let me see you here again.' Something urged her to have the last word.

But even that was to be denied.

'If you're here,' he tossed back, 'you can bet on that!'

Furious now, Peta called childishly, 'Also I don't think much of your judgment. Fancy, whom you've been looking over, is not for sale, he's simply my mount.'

That should silence him. No horse man likes his blood judgment questioned. That barb should hit home.

But the man turned briefly ... he was making no secret of his need to get back to the sale.

'You know what,' he said hatefully, 'I don't think much of Fancy's judgment, either. But then he's dumb and does what he's told. Poor horse!'

That would have been bad enough had not the next moment his rather drawling voice called from between the buildings where he had emerged to the sales a clear, 'Five thousand.'

'Six.' Peta recognized that as Mr. Mason from the neighbouring stud.

She did not go in to watch. She just stood and listened, listened horrified. Even before the final bid . . . which was from *him* . . . she knew the identity of the bidder.

Trentham. The man who had bought practically everything choice offered in the Kinrow Sales, the customer without whom Uncle Claud could not have emerged so cheerful, so inspired for further action down under, as he was.

And she had said: 'All right, mister, on your way.'

Thankful that she would not have the humility of meeting him again, that is if she kept a wise distance until the float took his last purchase off, Peta went her own . . . and faintly uneasy . . . way at once.

It was a joy to watch Uncle Claud basking in the success of the sale at dinner that night. It put that other humiliating happening out of Peta's mind. It came back, of course, with the name of Trentham, but until then . . .

'We've done handsomely, Peta.' Trust Uncle Claud to include her, Peta thought lovingly. 'Now we can start out in Tasmania in a proper, efficient way.'

'Then it is Tasmania finally?'

'Yes. I've consulted Australia House regarding the Commonwealth's varying climatic conditions, and the apple isle seems the place for us.'

'Is it an apple isle?'

'It produces some of the best apples, most prolific crops, in the world.'

'Fancy will like that,' smiled Peta.

'I'm liking it myself, girl. Even had I not been kicked out of Kinrow, it wouldn't have been the same here without Alice. I'll feel nearer to her over there. She was a wonderful person, Peta. We met rather late in our days . . . she was visiting England on her life savings . . . and it's hard for a woman in the maturer years to be a Ruth.'

'. . . "Whither thou goest, I will go . . . where thou lodgest, I will lodge",' nodded Peta, touched.

'Yes. Naturally she loved her own country, but she never went back. We often regretted, Alice and I, that it was the autumn of our lives instead of summer,' sighed Uncle Claud, 'and there could be no children. But you came along, Peta, and filled that void. Alice loved you.'

'I loved Aunt Alice. Like you, Uncle Claud, I'll feel nearer to her there as well, even if Mr. Gillett didn't enthuse over Tasmania. That is, for me.'

'Because of the likeness to England? Yes, I've been told about that. Towns called Bridgwater, Melton Mowbray, Tunbridge, Kempton. Taverns with signboards swinging in the breeze with names like Rose and Crown, Dusty Miller, Wheatsheaf, Harvest Home. Peta girl, will it be too like home, as Gillett said? The scenery might be like your own Cornwall. There's also a Launceston on a Tamar River.'

'Probably named by a nostalgic newcomer,' suggested Peta. 'No, Uncle, as I said to Mr. Gillett: "I've turned a page".'

'Good girl,' he awarded, then, to divert her, to stop the tears obviously pricking her eyelids, he related the sales' highlights, some amusing, some epic . . . especially that tussle between Mason and Trentham. Trentham, of course, had won.

'Of course,' Peta said. 'Money always wins.'

'Money wisely used generally does. This Trentham has timing and perception.'

'He's American, isn't he?'

The telephone was pealing. It had barely stopped since the end of the sale . . . cronies of Uncle Claud ringing him up to congratulate him on a successful disposal.

'Yes, Peta. At least he's off back there again, to Kentucky, though the purchases, I believe, and he himself eventually, I've heard, are going to— Who is it this time, Jean? Old Watson? Yes, I'll have a natter with him.'

Peta helped Jean with the dishes, and by that time the natter was over and Uncle was eager to discuss plans.

'You're to leave almost at once on the *Amory*, Peta, it's quite a modern cargo ship, I'm told. I'm sorry it can't be a passenger liner, girl, with all a liner's social attractions, but there were Omar, Brilliant Bess and Fancy to think of, and passenger liners don't go in for stock.'

'Uncle, I'd prefer to go that way even if I didn't have Omar, Bess and Fancy ... but what about the others?'

'Just as I figured to you before, Peta. You go ahead on the *Amory*, get our fellows safely there, then while they serve their quarantine you fly back for the next bunch. Three on a ship is enough for any stablehand.'

'I could handle more.'

'It will be enough. We'll have them to start off with while the second batch serve quarantine.'

'When will you come, Uncle Claud?'

'I'll fly out in time to see Sebastian, Meridian and Fair Flash ... yes, those three are my choice for a second consignment ... off the ship for their stint of detainment, and to help you kick off with Omar and Bess.'

'You're not including Fancy,' she pointed out.

'Fancy's family,' he grinned. 'The ship leaves on Friday week. All right with you, girl?'

'Splendid. I must have known when I got those vaccination shots for my cruise this year. It's only a matter now of packing my bag. And there'll be no sad farewells, either. I'll be back in little over a month.'

'Yes, the *Amory*'s a fast ship and is going via Africa direct. I'm sorry about that as regards ports for you, Peta, but I'm pleased for our cargo.'

'Ports are exciting,' agreed Peta, 'but the sea is the sea, isn't it?'

'A good slant when you're going to be surrounded by it in Tasmania.'

'Uncle Claud, we're surrounded by it here.'

'Of course.' He ruffled her hair fondly. 'I'm not functioning too sharply. Fact is I'm tuckered. I'm going to turn in, Peta, I'm not nattering to anyone else about the sale.'

'Even – Trentham?' Now *she* was bringing it up.

'He was flying out tonight. He'd be on his way to the

14

States by now.' Uncle gave another ruffle, yawned and went out.

'Wa-all,' imitated Peta of the westbound Trentham, 'I've no argument over that!'

The *Amory* left on the appointed Friday. It sailed in the high tide because of its big cargo – 'But you're above the Plimsoll line, Peta,' Uncle Claud assured her. 'I don't know what kind of cargo,' he went on. 'It could be peacocks or cheap tin trays. But I do know there's more horses than our horses, and the appropriate attendant for them.'

'How many passengers are there, Uncle?'

'Under twelve, I expect, so as not to require a doctor. Did you like your cabin, Peta?'

'It's splendid. So are the quarters for Omar and Bess and Fancy.'

'I've had a long chat with the Captain. He's a horse-lover, so I think you'll have every co-operation there. Now' – watching the hatches closing and all the gangplanks except one being lifted away – 'I think I hear the flutter of the Blue Peter. Any questions, girl?'

'None. I just settle the horses in quarantine and fly back again.'

'The air ticket is arranged. You have only to fix the date. I would have done that, too, only the timing of a cargo vessel is not always predictable. Well, goodbye, Peta, good trip and see you soon.'

That 'see you soon' took any sting out of the farewell, though, Peta thought sensibly, how could there be a sting when it was so brief a parting?

'See you soon, Uncle Claud.' She kissed him, walked to the gangplank with him, kissed him again, then, because she knew he would not move from the wharf while she waited on deck, and because there was a cool breeze which was not for elderly country gentlemen unaccustomed to rude sea air, she went to her cabin.

It was truly a splendid berth, fully serviced, and even with a minute sitting-room of her own. Its scheme was her favourite muted gold, not her favourite because of her own

15

deep gold colouring, dark honey hair, goldenish eyes, faintly apricot skin, but instinctively, as autumn was, as topazes and ambers were, as yellow roses and burnished clouds were, something very near to her heart.

The stewardess came in to ask if she wanted anything.

'Everything's lovely. I'm very pleased. When do we sail?'

'But we've left,' laughed the stewardess. 'I'm not surprised you didn't notice, this is a very smooth ship.'

'How many passengers?'

'Six, and the other five are men.'

'Well,' shrugged Peta, 'at least I have one kindred soul. I believe there are more horses aboard, consequently another attendant.'

'Yes, but his steward isn't happy about him. He doesn't look at all well, poor fellow.'

'Sick so soon?'

'Not seasickness, he was off colour before he came on board. He said he would have bowed out, but the trouble didn't start until the twelfth hour. It's always the case, isn't it?' The stewardess bustled out.

Peta went down to check Omar, Bess and Fancy, and found them quite comfortable. She declined an offer from an elderly gentleman to whom she was introduced by the Captain to take a nightcap, and, because it had been rather an arduous day, went to bed.

Breakfast the next morning was brought to her, and she revelled in the luxury. But she wasted no time in dressing and going down to her charges, still content and comfortable. After that she took a turn round the ship, found a protected deck chair and settled to read a book. The gentleman of last night joined her with two others of the same vintage, and they talked until lunch.

'Two to go,' smiled Peta to the Captain over that meal ... she was referring to their numbers ... and the Captain answered, 'One is confined to his berth; this Mr. Andrews, the other stable attendant, is unhappily not at all well. But here's our Mr. Travers.'

Peta glanced up, and liked what she saw. A tall slim man, refreshingly nearer her own age than the other passengers, blue-eyed, fair-haired, smiling, was approaching the table. But more important than looks was the man himself. He was nice, she felt sure of it. She found herself smiling quickly in response to the bright quirk he had flashed at her. They began to talk at once.

At the end of the meal, benevolently nodded out by the older passengers and by the Captain, Peta went instinctively to the deck with Peter Travers.

'And you're Peta, too,' he said, and he gave a little bow. He said it as though it was a secret seal between them, and put out his hand.

In the days that followed to Las Palmas, but only past Las Palmas, for it was a direct ship, Peta supposed it was only natural that she and Peter Travers sought each other's company.

At least that was what she told herself; her heart said something else. It was not the glamour of shipboard life ... for the cargo boat had all and more of the luxuries of a passenger liner ... it was Peter himself. She warmed to him at once. In an atmosphere of calm turquoise seas, for the weather to the Canaries had been wonderfully kind, with nights of pearl and deep sapphire to complete a jewel box, it was no wonder she watched for his coming every morning, sat late on the deck with him at night. But still it was more than that, she knew. It was Peter – Peter himself.

She had never known such a sense of instant companionship and closeness. A little bewildered at the quickness, at the completeness of her feelings, once she actually asked her heart: Is it because unconsciously I waited for a Peter that I'm happy like this?

He was a very relaxed person, never curious about her, nor revealing much of himself.

Because the other stable attendant was still unwell, there was no one with whom Peta could talk shop. At times she would have liked to have discussed the sea legs of Omar, Bess and Fancy, but after a few sentences to Peter she had known he was barely listening.

Once, a little reproachfully, she had demanded, 'Peter,

don't you hear me?'

'Sorry, Peta. No, my dear – well, not much.'

'Then what do you hear?'

'Only the song I want to hear.'

'Song?' she queried.

' "If a man does not keep pace with his companions perhaps it is because he hears a different drummer; let him step to the music which he hears".'

She had looked gently at him, at the lean, rather delicate face, the dreamer's eyes. Yes, she had thought, Peter *would* hear a different drummer. She put away an errant suspicion that Uncle Claud would have found another quotation.

'Up and doing,' was more for Uncle Claud ... which reminded her, for all the shining turquoise of the sea, the barely ruffling quality of an almost tender breeze, she must see to Omar and Bess and Fancy.

But everything was right and they still were showing no effects. She nuzzled each in turn, then gave an extra nuzzle to Fancy.

The *Amory* started down the African coast, travelling closer than the passenger routes, close enough to make the huge continent beckon tantalizingly and frustratingly, but also affording diversion in the busier shipping life now that the Suez Canal had been closed.

While pleased about the diversion because of the absence of ports, Peta knew she really needed no diversion, not when there was Peter. They would lie in deck chairs side by side and he would speak of the places in which he had travelled, not the usual countries-faraway talk, but Peter's version ... softly-coloured, dreamy, romantic.

The night he kissed her Peta knew she had been waiting for it. She stood in his arms, unaware that in actuality, for all her twenty years, she was a quite inexperienced girl, falling in love with the first young man she really had met, *properly* met, that she was in a dream world of happiness, the sort of dreams that belong only to that young ... inexperienced ... girl.

'I love you, little Peta.'

'I love you,' she said back.

There was no need to talk about the future, what he did, where he was going, how it would entail her. The sea remained blue. The breeze remained tender. And the days, intoxicating days, spun on.

It was on the long run to the Cape that the Captain asked something of Peta.

The attendant to the other travelling horses was still ill ... the Captain's expression was a little concerned ... but fortunately to date there had been no trouble with his stock. One of the crew had been attending the stable, but this morning he had come up with the disquietening news that a mare was looking droopy.

'I thought, Miss Milford, you might look in when you go down.'

'Of course,' Peta assured him.

Once below she noticed that the ship was beginning to roll a little, and she bit her lip. Her uncle had tutored her well about horses on sea trips, unfortunately they were as prone as humans to the sensation of motion, but more unfortunately still they had not the therapy of being able to retch. She could only hope that Omar, Bess and Fancy had more or less become accustomed to the slight roll even on a calm day down here, and when she saw them her hopes were fulfilled. They looked fine.

Having brushed and watered them, sat a while and talked as horses like being talked to, she gave the usual nuzzle, closed them up, then went to the adjoining enclosure.

What met her eyes shocked her. Not the condition of the horses ... though the mare did look unhappy ... but the *identity* of them.

To an ordinary person a horse was a horse. Perhaps a white star on a brow might afford identification, a particular hue, but Peta needed nothing like this to recognize familiar Mr. X, Little Bruce and Dixiebell. They were Kinrow productions. If her memory served her right they had gone under the hammer to the tune of five thousand each. Gone to – *him*. To Trentham. Then what were they doing here?

She looked curiously around the enclosure and saw imprinted: Goa. Goa, she knew, was Indian . . . Portuguese Indian, so the owner, with such a name, probably was too. Uncle had told her there was keen Indian, Asian and Eastern interest in blood horses and in racing. Poor 'boys' and poor 'girl', she pitied, it would be a long journey where they were going. With Suez opened they would be there by now. She wondered why they had not been sent overland, or alternatively by air. Then second to her pity came resentment. She had pictured these Kinrow productions now in the lush blue grass country of America – with Mr. Trentham, admittedly, but enjoying what they had enjoyed at home. Instead that false pretender with all his thousands had only been buying to sell again. Angry beyond measure, she went across to Dixiebell, and found her anger, if possible, mounting higher. The mare on closer scrutiny was definitely seedy, not far from ill.

She spent all that day with Dixie, doing the things she had been taught had to be done, but the weather had worsened and the mare was nervous as well as nauseated. To make it worse, when she looked in at her own trio, they were not as bright as before . . . in fact they verged on the lacklustre. Not seriously, though, not like Dixie, more a simple instance of actually finding their sea legs for the first time, since the weather prior to this had been as calm as a Kinrow spring.

Concerned, though, for the other mare, Peta went to the Captain and asked to see the sick attendant to seek his advice. But the Captain had troubles of his own . . . the man was in a bad way . . . they were going to increase the speed and make a call at Cape Town after all to put him off. As Miss Milford knew they carried no doctor as they did not have the required number of passengers aboard, and the Captain did not like to take the risk of keeping to his direct route.

Peta had wanted to talk with the attendant on another subject other than Dixie's illness. She had wanted to know if this Mr. Goa always dealt with Mr. Trentham of the

United States. If the American always bought to re-sell. If he – However, she had no opportunity, for the weather became worse, and she became a very busy girl.

It was a bad three days to the Cape. The ship tossed. Dixie suffered. The other horses lost their gloss and verve. Also the stablehand, she learned, had to be watched every hour. All this while Peter ... though in fairness she could not blame him, this was not his 'song', as he had said ... remained frankly bored whenever, worried and concerned, she talked to him about her job, so unmistakably bored, indeed, that ruefully she put her problems – when she was with him, anyway – aside.

But it came to an end at last. The seas regained their glassiness, the wind its tender ruffle, and the *Amory* put into Cape Town and the sick man was taken off.

It was not until Peta and Peter had returned from Table Mountain and Lion's Head and the ship was putting out again that the Captain told Peta he had been in radio touch with the stud owner. He had been upset over the incident, he related, but very pleased that the man had been put ashore for treatment. He was grateful to the other stable attendant aboard for attention rendered, and tendered his thanks.

'Indian, isn't he?' asked Peta.

'No, not Indian.'

'But Goa—?'

'But that's not the – Ah, this was what I wanted.' The Captain took up the radio message the steward had brought.

'The fellow's all right, thank heaven. They operated ... and successfully ... at once. It was a twisted bowel loop. I ask you, where would we have been?' The Captain was so pleased at his own escape as well as the patient's that Peta did not break into his relief.

It still puzzled her, though, that the horses, like Kinrow's, were going through to Australia, for while attending to the other consignment she had ascertained that. Surely it would have been easier to tranship them from Durban then up the east coast.

'Perhaps,' said Peter disinterestedly when she forgot herself and said this, 'they're going to be raced first in Australia. There are quite a few Asian syndicates there.'

'Perhaps,' Peta agreed, stifling a faint resentment at Peter's boredom.

With that endearing, rather boyish way of his, he must have sensed the pique, for he leaned across and reminded her, 'The drummer, darling, and the different song.'

'What song do you hear, Peter?'

'You.'

'That's sweet, but – but there has to be more, hasn't there?'

'Has there?' he teased back.

How could she not smile up at him?

There were thousands of miles to Fremantle, and after that there were many miles more around the southern coast, but the sea, even in the notorious Bight, retained its mildness, and Dixibell, who had completely recovered with the recovery of the weather, blossomed again, with the rest.

The ship did not touch any of the capitals. It was to discharge its cargo at Sydney, and it went directly there.

Many times on deck under a moonlit sky Peta and Peter discussed their journey's end. Peter had been horrified when he had learned that Peta was to fly straight back to England.

'Why not?' she laughed. 'I've had a month of lazing.'

'But, darling, I can't lose you now. Look, I'll come, too.'

'But I start off all over again almost immediately. It's all right with me, it's my work, but, Peter, for you it would be unnecessary expense.'

'Nothing is unnecessary if it keeps me with you, Peta.'

'It's still quite feckless.' Somewhere deep in her Peta was thinking of Uncle Claud's reaction. A kind man, even a sentimental one, he had a fund of plain common sense. And this proposal of Peter's made no sense. Especially when, a few minutes afterwards, Peter admitted that of course he would have to call upon her for financial help.

'I'm threadbare, quite frankly. I couldn't find the money.

But, darling, there's no pride in true love, so if you want me along with you, say the word.'

'I say the word, Peter, but I couldn't raise that much money either. Not your air fare back to England, your passage again out here. Also, my ship berth is booked already. You have to get in early with a cargo ship that accepts livestock as well. I'm sorry, Peter, I'm terribly sorry.'

His lips were in her dark honey hair, he was saying, 'I'm sorry, too, my darling, you see' . . . mock-seriously . . . 'I'm not the sort to be left behind.'

'What do you mean, Peter?'

There was a silence, then Peter laughed, 'I'm joking, of course. I'll be here waiting for you when you come back.'

'It won't be long. Little more than five weeks. Time to see Uncle Claud, embark again, and repeat the performance.'

'Honey, don't you dare!' Now he was biting her ear in warning. 'Don't you dare repeat this performance.'

'Oh, Peter!'

'Oh, Peta!'

It finished on that note.

She had a vague idea he was joining a paper. Journalism . . . or illustrating . . . would suit Peter. It didn't occur to her to find out any details. She loved him, and that was all that mattered – that, and the next month finding wings.

The horses settled in quarantine, she found wings herself within a day. Sydney looked enticing, but the sooner she left it the quicker she would be back . . . to Peter.

Darwin . . . Singapore . . . Bangkok . . . Karachi . . . they came and went like a dream. Then she was in London Airport, and Uncle Claud was waiting for her, and looking fine.

—Afterwards she was to ask herself *did* Uncle Claud look like that, or did I still wear my rose-coloured glasses, my glasses that Peter gave me, that made everything so perfect, so idyllic?

Kinrow was knocked down now, related Uncle Claud . . . he did not want Peta to go out and she didn't, either.

They stayed at a London hotel, he briefed her on her second ferrying . . . 'a larger ship this time, Peta, some fifteen passengers and a dashing doctor. No falling in love!

23

I'll need you, girl.'

'There'll be no falling in love.' Peta added softly to herself, '*Now*.'

It was arranged that Uncle Claud fly out in five weeks' time. In that way he could conclude his lengthy legal business. 'After all, I suppose it's to be expected it's taking so long. I've lived all my life in England.' He added that he figured that this would coincide, more or less, with Peta's arrival in the *Roslyn*.

'And then, my dear, the quarantine for Omar, Bess and Fancy should be relaxed, and we can start off afresh.'

Yes, said Peta ... torn for the first time, really, and yet, she thought, I should have considered all this before, Uncle so very practical, such a man of the outdoors, Peter so – well—

The *Roslyn* left the next week. It was a bright, almost hot day when it edged out, so this time Peta remained on deck and waved to Uncle Claud until she could see him no more. The atmosphere was gay around her ... the other passengers promised a bright trip out ... Las Palmas was to be a scheduled call this time, no mere passing it by ... later Cape Town and Durban ... once in Australian waters every capital port.

So why, wondered Peta, suddenly shivering in the sunshine, did that cold finger touch her heart? But it would be Peter not being with her on this journey. Yes, it would be Peter.

It was an uneventful trip. Pleasant, but to Peta, anxious for journey's end, and with no problem from her charges to take her mind off herself, for her threesome travelled even better than Omar, Bess and Fancy, with no especial interest in the interesting ports since she had only one port in view, a little boring.

Then they were entering Sydney Harbour, the vast panorama of beach, bay and promontory unrolling on either side ... leaving the more elegant berths for a utilitarian haven in Johnston's Bay where the cargo boats tied up ... and Peta, with the rest of the passengers, was watching, searching—

Because it was a merchant wharf, there were few to greet the *Roslyn*. Peta could have counted the number on the dock with her two hands. And not one finger was for Peter.

There must be some mistake. The ship could not have been scheduled. Or it had come in earlier than expected. Or it was later than advertised. Peter had gone home and would return. Or again he had taken a job in the country . . . he had told her he liked to get around . . . and he would come down as soon as he could. Or—

She attended the horses, saw them on the floats and then followed the van to the quarantine.

Omar, Bess and Fancy were thriving. It might need the soft rains of Ireland and the limestone of Kentucky to put lustre on a horse, but the crisp Sydney winter, a winter still with a feel of spring in spite of that crispness, revelled Peta, obviously suited her 'boys and girl'.

'Their sentence will be up,' smiled the attendant, 'pretty soon, Miss Milford. In fact, next week.'

She saw Sebastian, Meridian and Fair Flash settled, then came back to the hotel that Uncle Claud had arranged. Uncle Claud, she had also been advised, would be coming on Wednesday's flight.

It was Monday now. She had planned to spend the time between with Peter, talking about their future, about Uncle Claud, of how Peter must come halfway to the old man – 'Oh, yes, darling,' she had heard herself reproach him lovingly, 'I know you don't bother about such things, I know you have different thoughts, I know you hear only your song, but you are both dear to me, so there!'

She had planned this . . . planned a hundred things. She would not cajole Peter, she would not argue with him, she would just spill her love, and love would do the rest.

But where was he to receive her love? Why hadn't he met her? Why hadn't he written? She had sent out a list of ports, but there had been no letter. Of course cargo ships were not always on time. Though . . . and something uneasily nibbled inside of her . . . the *Roslyn*'s schedule had been right up to the minute.

Perhaps he would be at the hotel waiting for her. She had written out the Fortescue. He would have missed meeting the ship ... typical of Peter ... so rushed round to where she was to await Uncle Claud.

But Peter was not there.

There would be a message at any moment. A bellboy paging: 'Miss Milford ... phone call for Miss Milford. Would Miss Milford come to the desk?'

There was nothing.

But in the morning there *was* something, and had her fingers not shaken so much that the print was a little blurred, Peta would have noticed that Overseas imprint and known it was not from Peter but Uncle Claud.

Yet not Uncle Claud. Nor would there ever be a cable from Uncle Claud.

REGRET TO INFORM YOU CLAUD MILFORD SUFFERED HEART ATTACK STOP DIED MONDAY STOP LETTER FOLLOWING STOP

GILLETT

CHAPTER TWO

UNABLE to wait until she returned to her room, Peta had opened the cable immediately. Now she stood unsteadily, in unreality, a little island of pain in the sea that was the buzzing foyer of the city hotel.

Uncle Claud gone from her! It seemed impossible. He had looked so fit, so full of enthusiasm, standing on the wharf ... or had that been because she only had seen him in her own happy haze, not as he actually was?

Her fingers clutched the cable so tightly it tore. She looked down on it again to make sure she had read it correctly. It was in two pieces now and she pieced them shakingly together.   Regret ... Claud Milford ... heart attack ... died Monday ... letter following. Even crumpled in two halves the message jumped out clear.

26

The supervisor at the reception desk, a keen, mature man with every guest in the vestibule in his sharp focus, was crossing quickly to Peta.

'Miss Milford, I think you have bad news.'

'Yes.' Peta did not know how she answered him, but she heard her voice adding, 'My uncle ... he's ... I can't realize it ... I mean ...'

'Miss Quinn will take you to your room.' Without moving from Peta's side the man signalled the receptionist. 'We'll send up tea. You mustn't come down for meals, they will be brought to you. Would you like the hotel hostess to sit with you? Perhaps an older guest—'

'I – I would like to be alone.'

'Of course.'

Miss Quinn made her comfortable in a chair by the window; when the tea came she put it on a small table within reach. Then she left quietly. But as soon as the lift clicked Peta got up from the chair and began walking round, picking up objects, putting them down. The tea grew cold.

Uncle Claud had gone. He had said once that she had filled a void, but who would fill the void left by that dear old man?

It seemed unbearable to her that he had not even been spared to come to Australia, to his Alice's country, where, he had said, he would feel nearer to the wife he had loved so much.

Everything seemed so purposeless now. The effort of cataloguing the stud, of engaging the auctioneer, the week of strain and anxiety, for a successful sale meant so much. Then the arranging for Omar and Bess and Fancy, Peta's passage, the flight back, the repeat performance with the next three. All for what?

It wasn't fair! Peta clenched her fist and hit into the pillow. She was lying down now, anxious for the grief that would relieve her but seemed reluctant to come.

If only she had Peter here! Peter could start the healing tears. He was so gentle, so compassionate. There was nothing roughshod about him. He was all sympathy ... even if,

27

and she knew this was the case but forgave it, the real interest was not there. Yet he had admitted abstraction, admitted it honestly. He also . . . and her chin tilted a little . . . had spoken his love. The second outweighed the first, Peta thought, it was love that counted. Oh, Peter, where are you? I need you.

It was growing darker, but she did not put on the light. It's my fault he has gone, she thought, I should have helped him before I flew back. He said he had no money, how could I expect him to remain here in a big city just waiting my return? He's tried for a post, been unsuccessful and left. He'll come back, I know it. But I want him *now*. I want someone to turn to. Someone to – to –

There was a tap on the door and her meal came. Later on it was removed.

She got through the night . . . she could not have said how . . . and the next morning she went downstairs.

'You're feeling a little better, Miss Milford?' asked the supervisor sympathetically.

'Yes, thank you. You've been most kind.'

'We've been very unhappy that the news reached you here . . . that it had to come at all. I see you're going out. That should help. It's a lovely day.'

'Yes, I – I thought I'd walk.'

Walk and look . . . look for Peter. He might not have gone after all, he might have forgotten the day of her return, the name of the hotel.

She did walk and she did look, but of course it was useless. She had known it would be, but she couldn't help herself.

Then, after lunch nibbled in a park, she went to the quarantine, urged on by a longing just to stroke Fancy, Fancy whom Uncle had bought because he liked him. 'For a horse man that's reason enough.' It was benison to rest her head against the big grey shoulder, wet the shining skin with the first of her tears. Perhaps Fancy understood . . . Peta did not know . . . but he stood very still.

The attendant reported that the next three had settled nicely.

'Have you made arrangements for the others, miss?'

'No, not yet.'

'Well, I'd begin if I were you. They're due out tomorrow, and after the term is up there's an extra fee. Fair enough, there'd be a fee wherever you stabled them. I'm just telling you so you can think it out.'

'Thank you, I shall think it out.'

Think, think, think ... She wished she could, but she felt numbed, unreal, not here.

'I'll wait for Mr. Gillett's letter,' she decided, grateful to have something definite in view. 'If I know Gilly he'll have written at once.'

She was right. The air-mail awaited her the next morning.

'Dear Peta' ... Mr. Gillett had been her father's friend, so there was no ceremony here ... 'this letter is almost as painful to me as it is to you. The only comfort I can offer is the hackneyed one that he did not know any pain, yet actually, Peta, this was so. It was a fine day and he was in the sunlight and death came to him, one could say, like a breeze taking a leaf from a tree.

'No doubt you are fretting that he never got to his wife's country, which he desired so much. But he was a fine man, and I've no doubt he is in that country now.

'Well, I must leave that and be practical. Forgive me if I intrude too soon with my humdrum talk, but there are things that must be said.

'As you are well aware, having been at the scene, the Kinrow sale was a complete success. However, the expenses that have accrued since then are quite staggering. The transport of the selected horses goes into four figures. Your own double journey made quite an inroad. The price of the acquisition of the Tasmanian property was considerable, while the usual taxes for the winding up of the old here and the stamp duties for the purchasing of the new there, again diminished the profits.

'On top of all this came your uncle's sudden passing. As you already unhappily know, Peta, death is an expensive business in England. I haven't gone into it all in detail, but I am certain the duties will be crippling to anyone starting out in a new venture in a new land. Yes, my dear, you are the sole inheritor.

'In this case, I am urging you to put your estate on the market at once, to sell even at a much lower price, then return to where the amount, although not a large one, will at least augment what you can earn yourself. Much better this, Peta, than the worry of a project that, quite frankly, needs twice ... thrice ... the money that I believe you finally will receive.

'No doubt you will be inclined to argue that your uncle would have faced the same problem, but he was very experienced. Also, of all the debits that have accrued, the cost of his dying is the one that has really counted.

'You will be assured of a position here. You know how I wanted you in the office after your parents' death.

'Forgive me once more for speaking practically at a time like this, but put it down to the fatherly concern of

Henry Gillett.'

For quite a while Peta stood looking down on the city traffic, but it was not to give herself time to think, to consider, but to word the letter she intended to write back to the solicitor.

She had no intention of returning to England to work in his office, but he was a kind man and she wanted to convey it in a kindly manner. But she also wanted to say it definitely and for all time, to put dear Uncle Claud's 'Pen-pushing for a Milford!' in a polite but beyond-argument way. To suggest that, as well as there being sentiment in her reason for stopping in Australia because it had been Aunt Alice's country and she, Peta, felt she owed this to Uncle Claud, it was a practical decision.

It took some planning. She found herself mentally inserting absurdities like: 'How could I leave Fancy?' ... Incredulities like: 'How could I leave Peter?'

But at last she had a reasonable draft and she sat down and wrote.

30

And it must have been fairly convincing, for three days later ... Peta still waiting at the hotel ... came a cable with an agreement.

HAVE NOTED DECISION STOP WILL HASTEN LEGAL BUSI-NESS STOP IF CHANGE OF HEART DO NOT HESITATE TO RETURN STOP BEST OF LUCK STOP

GILLETT

So her leap in the dark was started.

One thing, Peta thought wearily, the decision, and what it entailed, left her little time to grieve for Uncle Claud ... to think about Peter. Also, because of the fulfilment of their quarantine and the necessity of removing Omar and Bess and Fancy, of any second thoughts, as Mr. Gillett had hinted, nor of any preview, before she actually burned her bridges behind her, of the scene of her future operations. No, it had to be the horses and Peta Milford at that field of operation at the same moment, and, grateful for the ted-ious business of arranging transport, business that stemmed tears and delayed regrets, Peta spent the next few days preparing to leave the mainland for the little island in the south.

She knew nothing at all of Tasmania, but upon inquiry was told that it would be better for both the horses and herself to travel overland to Melbourne and then go on from there to Launceston.

'This place of yours,' she was informed, 'is near the West Coast, so proceeding to Hobart would only entail a longer route.'

She had not listened as closely as she should to the smaller details, she had been thinking nostalgically of Cornwall's Launceston, Cornwall's Tamar River. Mr. Gil-lett had warned her about homesickness, she remembered. Well, she must steel herself, and forget.

She did forget in the worry of superintending the re-moval of the horses, in the bidding good-bye to the next three now detained for quarantine, to the following up of the float to the southern state, to the superintending of the two 'boys' and one 'girl' to the inter-island ferry, to catching the plane across herself so as to be sure to be there in good time to arrange for a float to meet them.

It was a smooth flight for Peta ... barely time for coffee and biscuits before the jet was putting down again, putting down in terrain that fairly tore at Peta's heart. For here was no sunburnt country, no land of sweeping plains; here was another England. Fields again, not paddocks ... fields under varying crops, or sometimes lying fallow, making a chequered pattern as the craft touched down. Sometimes tanglewood fences. Sometimes box-thorn hedges with red berries. A gleam of left-over snow in the hidden fold of a hill – or was it quartz winking back? Peta knew she would never know for certain, for her eyes were blurred with tears. But she recovered herself, collected her bags in the bright airport and took the bus into town.

Sydney Travel Centre had booked a Launceston hotel for her. She had only one night to put in, then she would meet the ferry at Bell Bay, see that the horses were comfortable in the float, then travel the same time as they did but in the small hire car that also had been reserved to ... Where was it again? She looked it up. She looked up the property that Uncle Claud had purchased and now was hers. Garo was its name. It conveyed nothing, except that it was brief and rather like the name of that person who had purchased the Kinrow strain from the man Trentham. Goa, she remembered, and this was Garo.

She could have circulated in the lounge that night, managed to glean a little of the district into which tomorrow she would travel, for the people here were friendly, she had seen that at once, but the likeness of the sparkling winter night to nights she had known at home, that crisp fresh feel of all cool countries, the clarity of the stars in a frosty sky, kept her in her room, afraid to open old wounds.

After early breakfast next morning she drove out in the small rented car to the ferry terminal, delighting in pine plantations, in sawmills milling myrtle and spilling dark sawdust, in a green river that changed to deep blue where it became trapped in twin headlands.

The horses had had a fair crossing, which was a relief,

for she had been warned about the Bass Strait and how it could blow up very rough. Quite unmistakably the cool air pleased them after their months in Sydney's more languorous climate.

Peta spoke with the float man and arranged that he take the lead. It was a goodish distance, he said, but not all that arduous. Nowhere in Tasmania was very far from somewhere else. And because of their prompt start they should make it by dusk.

It proved a glorious journey. After some miles and some hours, brilliant blue sea stayed most of the way with them on their right, until, in the early noon, they veered south, and then mountain, valley, lake and pasture flashed by like the facets of a kaleidoscope, so that Peta could not have said what ... apart from parts of England ... this country presented to her, only that it was breathtakingly beautiful.

It was well past dusk when they reached journey's end. But then it was winter and the night came early, a fact perhaps that the float man had forgotten. He was very good, though, opening up the house that suddenly loomed up in the darkness ... 'No trouble, miss, door was on the latch ready for you.'

She was a little surprised at that, but almost overwhelmingly delighted at the size and imposing appearance of the building. She had been prepared for some dismay. Mr. Gillett had not sounded too optimistic, and it was usually the way with pigs in pokes that they disappointed, never fulfilled. But this house, with its lights switched on, more than fulfilled. She had anticipated basic furniture, but not full furnishings, and lovely old furnishings, as met her eye.

Also the stables, the float man reported, very impressed, were most modern and commodious. He would put Omar, Bess and Fancy in for her.

She thanked him, paid him, watched as he started his float northward again. Then she turned back into the house. Two-storey, she delighted again, and went first upstairs to investigate.

The rooms were large and should be brightly sunlit by

day. The bathroom was quite modern. There was an air of occupancy, somehow. Evidently the last owners had left the residence quite recently. She was glad of that. A long empty house seems to acquire ghosts as well as dust.

Down to the kitchen ... and again an odd air of occupancy for all the strictly immaculate order. A foolish feeling that if you opened that refrigerator that food would be awaiting there.

She laughed at herself ... and then the laughter was receding. She had entered the large living room now, and though she had not opened the fridge for evidence, evidence fairly slapped her in the face at a fire burning in a grate.

A neighbour informed of her coming, perhaps? But if anyone did know, how would they know when?

Now she began to see *real* occupancy, not just sense it. A book deposited pages down, keeping a place. A hat hanging up. A coat on the back of a chair. She ran upstairs again and approached the bed. Nervously, unwillingly, she opened it up. It was made.

The bathroom once more. A towel hung there and she had not noticed it before. Even as she stared at it ... large and checked and essentially masculine ... a clock chimed.

She ran down again, then ran to the stables, ran by the kitchen path, not noticing she was entering a different barn from the one where the float man had indicated that he had lodged her two 'boys' and one 'girl'.

For a moment the truth did not dawn on her, then she realized she was *not* looking at Omar, Bess and Fancy but at stock belonging to someone else. Belonging to whom? What had happened? How was she here? And where and what was here? Was all this a nightmare?

Then her glance fell on a stable-mark, and she came nearer to the horses. Kinrow horses, she recognized. Sold that day to Trentham. Sold by Trentham to – To Goa? Mr. Goa? The Goa Stud? Well, Goa *something*.

But what was Goa stock doing in her stud? In Garo? What was –

Now Peta was standing still, icy still. As clearly as if she was speaking at this moment she was instructing the horse

34

float man in Launceston again. At Bell Bay. At the dock. Telling him ... telling him – Goa. GOA. She could hear her own voice:

'To Goa.'

Where, then, was Garo? How could she find it? What did she do until the morning when she could start looking for it? Where was the man who owned this place ... it had to be a man with that big checked towel. How soon would he come and discover his intruder? Too soon, she thought, remembering that waiting fire behind the fireguard.

She turned in panic and ran to the door, then, rising out of the dark it almost seemed, rising from nowhere, a figure loomed before her, caught her as she tried to escape. But it did not hold her, on the contrary it impelled her almost violently forward. A voice that vaguely registered even in her agitation, a slow drawl of a voice with a sounding of the final 'R', said, 'All right, boy, on your way!'

Almost the words she had used, she remembered, panic-stricken, to this man, this American, at Kinrow, and now being used ... she had travelled in jeans and was still wearing her peaked cap, so he had taken her for a youth ... to her.

But how was Trentham here in Tasmania, Australia? And would he ask a similar question of Peta Milford when he finally focused the lamp that he was raising now to see her face ... that is if he remembered her? Would he ask why she trespassed, what she was doing at Goa? For Goa must be a place, she realized now, not a name.

Then where was Goa? More important, where was Garo? *Her* place?

CHAPTER THREE

AFTERWARDS ... and it was to be a long time afterwards, as it happened ... Peta was to ask herself why she then had done the foolish thing that she proceeded to do. Had she thought about it, she would have known how ridiculous it was to think of hiding, of waiting for the man to shrug his shoulders over the affair and go back to the house. Then, after his house lights were switched off, and he presumably slept, for her to creep to the stable ... the *other* stable ... collect her horses and get away.

It had been such an absurd plan ... why, her clothes and handbag were still in the house, in fact, everything, except Omar, Bess and Fancy, that she possessed were in the house ... that she could have laughed at it lying there in bed. Lying? In bed?

But at the time it happened all she had thought of was escaping before he actually focused the light and recognized her ... she was presuming he had taken enough notice of her at Kinrow to remember ... and to prevent that she leapt up from where he had pushed her and kicked the lamp from his hand. She had heard him swear furiously, reach out to grab her this time, not just help her from his property, but the surprise of the action gave her an advantage, and she was off like a shot. Behind one of the barns, she thought. In a copse of trees. She would find somewhere.

She might have found it, too, and frozen to death in the Tasmanian winter night waiting for him to give up the search ... *if* he gave it up ... only the plan failed. In the unfamiliar darkness she ran into something ... a post, a tree, she did not know what, she was only aware of impact, of something very hard and hurtful.

When she woke up there was a lump on her head and a bandage round the lump.

And she was lying in bed.

She opened her eyes, closed them hastily, opened them again. It was daylight ... a daylight as brilliant as she had thought these large bedrooms would present. *These* bedrooms? Oh, no! She closed her eyes again.

Her head was aching mercilessly, but as she worked down from her head she forgot it. She was dressed in something very bulky, serviceable and definitely masculine. She held up an arm, but could not see her fingertips. The same with her legs ... her feet appeared to be well up in the pyjamas. Pyjamas? She possessed no pyjamas. She did more feeling, then she stopped. I'm in someone's pyjamas. In someone's bed. It was as simple as that.

There were steps. Probably the housekeeper who had got her into the pyjamas ... but why hadn't she used one of her nightdresses? Just in case it wasn't a housekeeper, though, Peta shut her eyes tight, leaving only enough room to win a narrow glimpse. It wasn't the housekeeper, it was *him*. She closed the thin space. If she kept still and 'asleep' long enough he'd go away, and then she could think, for even though her head protested, she had to think.

She heard him draw up a chair. No doubt now he was looking at her. The impulse to look back was almost unbearable. He was bending over the bandage, easing it a little and examining the wound. Now she could resist no longer. She permitted the slit again ... and there, an inch away, no more, an eye glinted back at hers. *His*.

'Open up,' he said.

At first she pretended oblivion, but she felt his hand on the shoulder of the pyjamas, by the size of them *his* pyjamas, and she hastily obeyed.

'Good morning, Miss Milford,' he said.

So he did remember. On the other hand he might have seen her name on her bag. Would she say, 'Good morning, Mr. Trentham,' in return?

She considered so long he said irritably, 'Don't pretend I'm that unimportant. Not to be aware of my name, I mean. You must have written me up in the accounts a dozen times at least.'

'I wasn't doing the books.'

37

'No, I recall. You were policing the stud.'

'Is there anything wrong in that?' she flashed.

'There's a way of approach, Miss Milford.'

She touched her head feelingly. 'You don't seem to know the approach, either.'

'Ah, but I wasn't trespassing.'

'Since when have buyers had the legal run of a property?'

'There are buyers,' he reminded her maddeningly, 'and buyers.' His tone reminded her just how much *this* buyer had bought.

'Actually,' she argued, 'I wasn't trespassing either.'

'In the dark of night in someone else's grounds?'

'I thought,' she said miserably, 'the grounds were Garo.'

'Garo?' he flashed in interest, and the flash encouraged her. He obviously knew about Garo, *her* Garo, which made it ... and unwillingly she conceded this, but after all this man was by no means a nobody ... fairly important. His next remark, though, deflated her.

'How the hell would you think Goa was Garo?'

When she did not answer, not liking to explain her absurd mistake of absentmindedness in directing the float to the wrong stud, he said derisively, 'How could anyone connect Goa and Garo?'

'Are they ... I mean ...'

'You mean are they different?' he said unfeelingly.

'Y-yes.'

'Then your answer is yes. Like chalk and cheese. You' – with a mean smile – 'are not the cheese.'

'But – but you knew about the place. You just said so ... or at least your eyes did.'

'Of course. Most people know their next-door neighbour.'

'Next-door?' Her spirits rose a little. This stud seemed so well situated, surely one in the near vicinity would share the benefits.

'Perhaps a translation of the names will answer you better than I could.' Now his voice was dry.

'Translation?'

'From the aboriginal. Yes, there were aborigines here

38

once. A smaller species than on the mainland. Also quite harmless, there's no evidence of any war weapon, neither boomerangs, woomeras or spears. That, we suppose, would be the reason the white man was too much for such a peace-loving race and that they died out.'

'And – and the translation?'

'Goa means west. That's where this stud is situated. This is the western part of the island of Tasmania.'

'And – Garo?'

'Lying down,' he said blandly. 'Another version could be – marsh. The chalk, you see, and the cheese.'

Marsh ... but it was impossible. Uncle Claud had paid a good sum for the property that he had intended making the new Kinrow. Uncle, though the kindliest of men, had been no fool when it came to real estate. He simply would not have parted up hard-earned cash on a worthless deal. She herself had used the phrase 'pig in a poke', but Uncle Claud would have only dealt with a well-established agent and in facts.

He was watching her face, reading her change of expressions, and he must have softened, for he said, 'Look, I'm exaggerating, it's not all that bad.'

'Nor all that good.'

'It would be as good as you paid. I know the man who was handling the property ... I should, for I was after it myself ... and old Finley is reliable.'

'Yes, his name was Finley. Then why didn't you buy it?'

'I was elsewhere at the time that Garo became actually available.' He added, 'America.'

'Presumably, being an American.'

'American?' He was raising his brows at her.

'Aren't you?'

'No. I'm an Apple Islander. Which means Tasmanian. What made you think ... Oh, I suppose it was the accent I picked up. Those rolled "R's".'

'And the drawl.'

'Crispness is not exactly an attribute of any Australian speech,' he corrected, 'so I will not be accused of acquiring a drawl.'

'Why must one acquire at all?' Her own voice was very crisp and English.

'It rubs off in America.' He rubbed his big hand through his hair and it fell back in a crooked parting. He added, 'Also I've been away more or less for years.'

'And all that time you wanted Garo?'

'Yes.'

'Then – then it can't be as – chalky as you say.'

'I wanted it because I wanted to expand, and the only way to expand properly is to continue. You ... Garo ... was my only continuation point.'

'The other side?'

'Crown land. Green belt. Not for private use.'

'So for more room the cheese would have to put up with the chalk.'

'Perhaps I shouldn't have said that.'

'Not of marsh?'

'It isn't. At least only in spots. The fact is it's a little lower, a little less endowed, a little less everything, for which' ... he looked at her directly ... 'you undoubtedly paid a little less cash.'

'I wouldn't say that.' Her small chin was up.

'You wouldn't know much about it, would you? Being a new-chum you wouldn't know what was a fair Australian sum, and what wasn't. I know the price paid and I can assure you it was reasonable enough. As well as assure you, I'll cheer you up by making an offer right now of your price plus one third on.'

'I don't need that sort of cheering. The fact that you're anxious for my property takes away the chalk in it for me, Mr. Trentham.'

'Ah, but you haven't seen it, have you,' he said with a maddeningly innocent grin. 'Anyway, what am I wasting time with you for? It's your uncle who counts ... though undoubtedly, from the way you continually entered his conversation at Kinrow, you can twist him round your little finger. Nevertheless he is the deciding factor, so let's change the subject until I can make my offer where it counts.'

'I'm afraid, then, it will have to be to me.' The pain of

he last week made Peta's voice stiff and unemotional.

'He's not coming out? Don't tell me he's putting a slip of a girl in control of his new project?'

There were a lot of things she could have flashed at him, but all she said was a bleak, 'He died.'

'He . . . Claud Milford?'

'Yes.'

'But he was on top of the world. A remarkably well preserved old gentleman, I thought.'

'Yes.'

The terseness of her replies must have reached him. He stopped talking and looked at her instead. Looked a long time. Then he touched her hand.

'Sorry.' It was all he said, but there *was* sorrow there, and she felt it.

'Look,' he said, 'I'll get some tea.'

He was back very soon with it, and nothing was missing. Peta thought of the well-kept house into which she had walked last night, believing . . . at first . . . that it was empty because it was so immaculate.

'You are fortunate in your housekeeper, Mr. Trentham.'

'Yes, Miss Milford.' He was pouring now.

She accepted the cup and a finger of toast, and said, 'Perhaps you could tell her to bring my clothes. I'm feeling quite well and I'd like to get up.'

'You can't do that.'

'Why not?'

'The doctor is coming.'

'There's no need for the doctor.'

'I'm the one to say that — after all, it was on my property that you received that egg on your head, and I don't want false claims made on me later on.'

'I won't be making claims, and I won't be seeing any doctor.'

'The doctor has been telephoned,' he shrugged.

'Then at least there is no need for me to remain in bed. Look, Mr. Trentham' . . . irritated . . . 'Garo might not be worth the seeing, but I still want to see it. Seeing you've rung the doctor I suppose I'd better not make a fool of you, but I'll save time now washing and getting dressed.' As he did not move she said sharply, 'So will you tell your housekeeper, please.'

'Tell her what?'

'To bring my clothes.'

'I'd prefer you to remain in bed. You seem all right, but concussion can be delayed.'

'Kindly bring your housekeeper.'

He did not move.

'Or,' continued Peta, '*I* will call for her.'

'By all means.' He still did not move.

'What's her name?' she demanded.

'Trentham.'

'Trentham?'

'Nat Trentham.'

'Natalie,' she concluded. She flashed him a mutinous look and opened her mouth to call, but he intercepted quietly with, 'Nathaniel, as a matter of fact.'

'Nathaniel? That's a man's name.'

'I am.'

'You .. you are your own housekeeper?'

'Yes. Anything wrong with that?'

As she did not answer, for her mind now was darting along another channel, and not liking where the channel led, he drawled, 'Don't tell me the English regard only the female of the species as suited for the domestic arts. Who inaugurated the gentleman's gentleman?'

'You mean—' ... her voice was small and faint ... 'there's no woman in the house?'

'No.' Now the direct look at her again. 'You're from swinging England, don't tell me you're queasy over things like that.'

'I'm not. But I am a little concerned over these – pyjamas.'

'What's wrong with them? Is it because they're American, not British, made?'

'No. But they are – on,' she stated flatly.

'Over,' he stated flatly back, 'a conglomeration of clothes. Do you always rug up like that?'

42

She was feeling surreptitiously, and at the same time feeling her cheeks go burning red. What a fool he must think her, and what a fool she had been not to have noticed before that he had only removed her shoes.

'I knew that extra warmth was essential,' he said bluntly. 'I thought my pyjamas filled the bill better than those flimsies that were all I could find in your port. I reckon your first move, Miss Milford, if you settle down in Apple Isle, will be to make the purchase of a thick flannelette nightgown.'

She was still red, and she felt a fool. She also felt that an apology to him was called for.

'I'm sorry,' she blurted, 'at first I thought—'

'Yes. And had I considered *that* necessary' – a significant pause – 'I would, of course, have attended to it, too. You would have done the same for me.' As she did not speak, he proffered with the hint of a grin, 'Look, I'm a vet.'

'Perhaps, but I'm not a horse.'

'I'm sorry,' he said rather bemusedly, 'that it all upsets you so much.'

'It doesn't. But it does upset me that you're thinking me a – a prude. I'm not, I'm a very sensible and down-to-earth person. People dealing with nature have to be. I'm not concerned for the reason you think I am but because I'm acting as though I am. I mean ... I mean ... well, for one thing I've gone red.'

'Pink,' he corrected gravely. 'Now, enough of all this. And will you please, seeing you feel you owe me something, lie back after all and wait for the doctor. Incidentally' – taking up the tray – 'it's a lady doctor.' His smile barely flickered. 'So—' He gave an indicative shrug.

'Is there a town here?' she inquired.

'Ten miles from here. On a small bypass from the Murchison Highway. We're on a remote road leading also from the Murchison, but in the opposite direction to Berribee.'

'Ten miles, you said. Then she won't be pleased coming out for nothing, for I'm perfectly all right.'

'Don't worry about it, Miss Milford, Helen Kemp and

I have an understanding.' With that he went out.

Either he had rung much earlier, or Doctor Kemp was a fast driver, for scarcely had he left the room than Peta heard a car pull up, then a voice ... a woman's ... call, 'Hi there, Nat!'

'Hi there, Helen. I've a patient for you upstairs.'

But it was a long time, or it seemed so, before Peta heard the lighter steps climbing the flight. Why not, she thought, when there's an 'understanding'?

When she saw Helen Kemp she understood that 'understanding'.

'Once,' Peta remarked feelingly as Helen briefly examined her, 'a girl had brains *or* a girl had beauty.' She looked with mock resentment at the doctor.

Helen Kemp put down her stethoscope, sat back on the bed, then brushed a strand of nut-brown hair from her forehead.

'I don't know about brains, but I do know about beauty. You must be concussed after all.' She smiled companionably at Peta. 'All the same,' she appreciated, 'coming from my own sex, I'm very grateful. One more or less expects it from a male.'

—Especially when that male has an 'understanding' with you, deduced Peta silently. Aloud she asked the doctor: 'Apart from my making odd statements, or so you say, how am I?'

'Nothing sprained, strained or broken, as far as I can judge.'

'Then I can get up?'

'No. You see, concussion is a touchy thing.'

'I'm not concussed.'

'I think you're right about that, but the fact is it could still be iffy. Injuries to the skull ... if you have sustained one ... take many forms. Even a small blow may tear a blood vessel, causing no disturbance for quite a while, and then trouble coming in a rush. There's only one in twenty suffer complications, but Nat did the right thing putting you to bed and sending for me.' As she was speaking, Doctor Kemp was drawing up a chair, making herself comfortable.

'What are you doing?' asked Peta, amazed.

'Watching you, of course.'

'But I wasn't watched before.'

'Most certainly you would be. I know our vet.'

'I don't like burdening you this way,' protested Peta.

'It's no burden, I've a day off and this will be a rest. Oh, I expect you'd sooner Nat, but—'

'I wouldn't.'

'No?' The doctor did not comment on that. Instead, she told Peta, 'We'll just keep you prone another hour or so, then that's that.'

'I'm anxious to see Garo,' protested Peta.

'Your property? Yes, Nat told me.'

So there had been conversation downstairs as well as 'understanding'.

'Can you tell me about Garo?' Peta begged.

'You'll be able to tell yourself about it quite soon,' advised the doctor. 'Close your eyes. Talk a little if you feel like it, but don't make bright conversation. Just drift. Be dull.'

'But I had a good night's sleep, I must have because—' She did not finish. She would have felt the same sort of fool as she had felt with Nat Trentham had she remarked that she could not remember about the pyjamas, so she pretended oblivion instead.

It was no pretence, as it happened. When she wakened again it was noon – Three hours of deep slumber. She couldn't credit she had slipped off, but she had. Doctor Kemp was perfectly satisfied and said so.

'Now you *can* get up.'

'Thank you.' Peta's voice was a little crisp.

She showered and dressed and came down to a lunch that the 'housekeeper' had prepared. As she might have known by now, it was an excellent one.

The three of them sat by the window for the meal. This was really the first time that Peta had seen her new home ground, for when she had arrived last night it had been dark. Now, in spite of herself, for to admire what she saw

45

was to admire Goa, the opposition one could almost say, she gasped aloud.

'It's all right,' said Nat Trentham laconically, evidently reading her thoughts, 'I have no exclusive rights on the backdrop.'

And a backdrop indeed it was. To the west were scallops of purple mountains. Nearer were pools of green shade on golden hillsides. Then came the fields ... no, she should think of them in Australia as paddocks ...

'Fields,' said Nat Trentham, again reading her thoughts. 'We're Australian in Tasmania but English variety.'

'It's pretty,' Peta allowed unwillingly; she was irritated because he had known what was in her mind again. She was more irritated a moment afterwards at his amused look at her discomposure.

'Pink,' he mouthed faintly, and she knew her cheeks were flushed.

'How is it to be home, Nat?' Helen asked, helping herself to salad.

'It's like coming back to a heart,' Nat answered briefly.

'It's really Nat's home,' explained the doctor to Peta, 'apart from those charming words.' She smiled at Nat. 'He and—' a pause. 'He's lived here all his life.'

'With that accent?' sniffed Peta.

'She likes things exact,' Nat informed Helen. To Peta he said: 'All my life barring some years here and there plus several days.'

'You don't count the hours?'

'I'll count them if you're particularly interested.'

'I'm uninterested.'

'Nat's father had this stud,' related the doctor, ignoring their interchanges, 'but it was not nearly as big as Goa is today. Or' – another smile at Nat – 'so I've learned.'

'The previous generation believed Tasmania was only suited for raising trotters,' Nat put in. 'I have different ideas ... especially now with Kinrow Blood.'

'And Kentucky blood,' included Peta, interested in spite of herself.

'That originally, too, was British. The best sires and

mares in the world come from England. Are you going to take a bow?'

'I'm not a horse.' This was the second time she had answered this.

Helen was laughing. 'You deserved that, Nat. America may have achieved you some new bloodstock and a roll to your R's, but it never imbued you with its smooth talk. You're still a native son.'

'It could be that Miss Milford likes the rugged type,' suggested Nat. 'What are your preferences, Miss Milford?'

'*Not* rugged,' she said so quickly that she surprised even herself. She had been thinking suddenly of Peter Travers, his lean, rather delicate face, his dreamer's eyes.

'Well, one thing, the lady knows her mind,' Nat observed drily. He glanced obliquely at Helen. '*All* the ladies present?'

Helen put down her knife and fork. 'That was a lovely meal, Nat.' Her voice was a little strained.

'Then aren't you finishing it?' There was an abrupt gentleness in Trentham's tone, a gentleness Peta would not have thought he had in him. She glanced at the doctor and was surprised at the sadness pulling at her mouth. It was gone in an instant, though, in fact it was so brief she was not sure it had been there at all.

'Thanks, Nathaniel,' Helen said, and began eating again.

'Who was in my uncle's . . . in my property before this?' Peta asked.

'Babworths. But they've been gone some years. That's why the place—' Nat, at a look from Helen, did not finish.

'Was it a stud?'

'Bread and butter only.' As Peta's eyebrows raised, he explained, 'They had no Cup dreams or anything like that, they just raised ordinary horses. Which, in case you don't know, are still needed.'

'I have one myself,' Peta said warmly.

'Name of Fancy.' His eyes glinted at hers.

'You have a long memory, Mr. Trentham.'

'It's necessary when you're dealing in pedigrees.' He

47

explained to Helen: 'I encountered Miss Milford in England.'

Encountered, thought Peta, was the word. 'Do you race?' she asked Nat Trentham politely.

'No,' he said politely back.

'But he might,' put in Helen, 'already he has changed from the trotters which were all his father went in for.'

'But not changed from breeding,' said Nat Trentham. 'Trotters or otherwise, it's the blood in my stock that I'm most interested in, not their racing potential, not a cup result.'

He said it so certainly and smugly, or so Peta considered, that she could not resist putting in a bland, 'One can always try another avenue.'

'I don't.'

'Isn't that dull?'

He was narrowing his eyes at her as he had from the door of Fancy's stable in Kinrow.

'I don't find it dull.'

'But perhaps you are.' – Why on earth was she baiting him like this?

'Meaning?'

'That one doesn't always have to be the same.' Remembering Peter, she added: 'You could hear a different drummer and step to a different song.'

She was suddenly sharply aware of an abrupt silence at the table. Looking at her companions she saw that the doctor's eyes were lowered to her plate, that Nat Trentham was looking through the window.

At once he looked back, though, and said quite shortly, 'If you've finished we'll drive over to Garo.'

'Not me, Nat.' It was Doctor Kemp.

'*You*, my girl,' he insisted to Helen.

'I have to get back to the surgery.'

'You have a day off. You said so.'

'I – I'll do the dishes.'

'All right, I'll give you five minutes, Helen. Meanwhile Miss Milford and I will look around the stables. Undoubtedly she will be anxious to see her – what was his

48

name?' He looked at Peta in cool inquiry.

'You recalled it yourself a moment ago,' she answered bluntly. But she got up all the same. She was eager to see Fancy.

But she did not see him ... for a while. Barely had they left the house than he swung her behind a tree, swung almost angrily. Turning furiously on her, putting his big hands on her shoulders, he asked, 'Why in hell did you have to say that?'

'Say what?'

'Say ... Oh, it doesn't matter.' His hands dropped away, but he still glowered.

'I don't know what you're talking about.'

'All right then, we'll leave it at that. Come on and I'll show you around.'

Looking back to Goa in daylight verified Peta's first impressions last night. It was a lovely old place ... roomy, comfortable, even elegant in its unstudied simplicity. There was a shabbiness, too, that she suspected was left that way to afford the mellowness of age, of good things bought in the beginning that grew old but remained good in proud usage.

She turned back again and skipped to catch up with him, for he had not waited but strode ahead of her when she had paused. The air was cold, but rather thrillingly so. It was a skipping, dancing sort of morning.

He was waving his arm to the different fields.

'In that western section I have my Kentucky fellers. I have my eye on Great Harry for Colleen. You'll see her in the enclosure we're rimming now. No need' – a laugh – 'to relate her home ties, not with a name like that.'

'Is Great Harry American stock?'

'American-reared only. He came from out your Kinrow way! Mason's stud.'

'England, Ireland and America now in Australia,' Peta remarked.

'The apple part of Australia, and in case you don't appreciate that, look over there.' He waved his arm to an orchard in the distance, bare now, but promising burgeoning of fat blunt buds later on, sweet largesse of fruit. For as far as Peta could see the apple trees reached up, skinny witches in winter, but she knew, debutantes in spring.

'And this,' he emphasized, 'is definitely not apple corner. That's a long way off, in the Huon Valley in the south, in the Mersey Valley in the north. In spring both places are a fairyland with their orchards spreading pink and white carpets over every hill and slope.'

'This would be bloodstock corner, then?'

'Good lord, no. Tasmania is not what you'd call a blue grass paradise. There's only a few of us in this business.'

'What, then?'

'Are you serious? I can see I'll have to give you a few lessons on this last and loneliest.' He began rolling a cigarette. 'Tassie is roughly divided into sections by virtue of terrain,' he told her. 'There are mountains through the centre and the West. That's why my people named this place Goa – West. That's us.' He lit up. 'We'll leave the more civilized east, the apple and crayfish happy hunting grounds and come west, young woman.

'It starts up north with potatoes and cows ... you'll do well to remember that, you're a bit stringy. Then it proceeds through semi-pastoral parts like this. Then through mining centres. Then through rugged mountain ranges still defying the explorer – and think on that, new-chum, in this present Year of Grace places still unexplored! And that's the truth. Down in our western corner there are more places than not where man has never set foot. It's said the rain forests to the coast are impassable. Trees have fallen through the ages and new trees grown out of them, and the process has been repeated for centuries until no one knows whether it's a horizontal or vertical jungle. But there are reports of fiords from circumnavigating boats, breathtakingly beautiful fiords, like nothing else in the world.'

'Please go on.' Peta was listening eagerly.

He seemed pleased at her interest, even though he had proved himself, she thought, a rather wandering native son.

'A quarter of a day from Goa and you reach Copper City, though it's more than copper now, of course.' He glanced

50

at her. 'Your name should be Katherine. You have the golden colouring of Queenstown. You could be Copper City Kitty. And in Queenstown you have a western frontier scene in a movie, played to the tune of changeover whistles at the smelting works of Mount Lyell.

'Well, enough of today's travelogue ... here are the stables.'

They turned in at the first barn.

Last night Peta only had had a vague impression ... and a favourable one ... of the stables. Now she found them very satisfactory – doors opening outwards and fastening back, abundance of light, abundance of sweet fresh air.

'There are special boxes for foaling. I have a mare waiting now. Also something I put in for myself – a comfy sitter's quarters near the foaling. It can be a trying time.' He exhaled and looked obliquely at Peta as he had before. 'Have you assisted?' he asked.

'Yes.'

'Have you done it alone?'

'No,' she admitted reluctantly.

'Well, Nature doesn't work on a bundy,' he reminded her rather brutally. 'I presume you know that.'

'Of course I know!' she snapped back.

He paused, then burst out as if he had to: 'How in tarnation with your inexperience do you hope—'

'I am not actually inexperienced.'

'But not actually experienced.'

'Look, Mr. Trentham, at least give me time. I didn't expect my uncle to – die.'

'Sorry,' he said sincerely as he had before.

When she did not comment ... and she couldn't have said a word, for her throat was choked up ... he waved to the house and suggested getting back as evidently Helen had finished the chores and was now waiting by the car.

But first Peta ran to the stable in which the float man had placed Omar, Bess and Fancy. She patted the other two but kissed Fancy, then came back feeling much better.

'Do we have to take a car to Garo?' she asked.

'Of course. It might be next door, but it's still some

eight miles.' They had come up to Helen now, and the two girls got in the landrover beside Nat, and he drove out of the gates and turned along a track.

There were hawthorn hedges on either side of the narrow winding way, and almost Peta could have cried out that just here she was in Devon. But no Devonshire cottage waited her at the bend of the track when Nat Trentham pulled up at last and drawled: 'Here you are.'

There it stood, as unlike Goa as ... well, as *he* had said. Chalk and cheese. It could almost, Peta thought unhappily, have had Chalk written on it instead of that distinct Garo ... the only really distinct thing about the place.

Perhaps it was functional, and she had no doubt that Uncle Claud being the practical person he had been would have made sure of that, but it was decidedly unlovely and very shabby. Not old elegant shabby but plain abandoned shabby. Windows needing repairs giving it a squint-eyed look. Eaves needing nailing making it appear awry. The rather sulphurous yellow it must have been painted once now the dingy colour of greying woollens.

She looked at the lumps in an old discarded garden, evidently shrubs once, but now tortuous shapes. She looked at barns, and they seemed dry enough, but oh, how dismally dark. She looked beyond to fields that ran rather steeply downhill, not rippled gently like Goa's. She looked at everything and everything was less, much less ... except that backdrop.

'Well,' said Nat Trentham still in that drawl of his, 'you have your first impression over, so let us see if we can't balance the account a bit.

'Now, the house is weathered, but, I would say, still weather-proof. We'll find out, anyway.' He held his hand out for the key.

The key? She had no key. She supposed ... too late at this moment ... it would come out with Uncle's things. Suddenly tears were stinging her eyes. She did not see in the tears Nat's quick glance to Helen, she only felt the doctor's hand on her shoulder.

When the tears cleared, she saw that Nat Trentham had

52

climbed through one of the squint-eyed windows and had opened the front door. He was holding it back for them to come in.

It was so dark that for a few moments Peta could see nothing. That was the first hard thrust. After the sunlight of Goa it angered her to think that Garo ... her Garo ... was so opposite.

'Windows can always be cut.' It was Nat Trentham's leisurely drawl, and her anger over the dismalness gave way to anger that once more he had guessed her thoughts. Why should he, this tall, estimating Australian with the narrowed eyes and the fingers performing their little rustle with paper and makings, why should he sense her like this?

Her own eyes were becoming accustomed to the gloom now, finding shape and reason. (Though, she thought, bitter again, extremely little reason.) For the room they had entered extended without any desirable preamble of entrance hall or corridor right to the exterior. Open the door, Peta despaired, and you would be actually within. A knock ... a response ... and the house would be a public place. For the rest, the room was low-ceilinged, long, and panelled in dark rough wood. It was completely bare and there was a smell of wet rot.

'It's a wet area, the west.' Again the man was keeping pace with Peta's thoughts.

The wooden floor was heaved and buckled and in one section there was actually a hole where the floorboards had rotted right away. Plaster had fallen from the ceiling and it lay like dirty snow on the floor.

In a room to the right, its window broken, thus letting in more light than the meagre glass in the main room, Peta could see a small fireplace, a sink and some empty shelves. But she crossed to the room on the left to begin with ... actually a shutter or two remaining here, slatting in thin grey bands of sun well diffused by dust.

'There is a staircase.' Nat's voice came in as dry as the dust on the shutters. 'A kind of attic bedroom. Perhaps, though, Miss Milford' ... she heard him making that rustling 'makings' noise again ... 'you'll bypass that as duly examined.'

The dryness of the words ... and the instinctive command he was taking ... irritated her. 'No,' she said stubbornly, 'I will not.' Her sharper focus now had seen the staircase to which he had referred ... she had not noticed outside that the building was two-storeyed ... and she walked firmly towards it.

'I wouldn't,' he intervened coolly but intentionally. 'It's years since the Babworths were here, and if I remember rightly they only used downstairs.'

He had put himself between Peta and the flight, and, as if he had challenged not advised her, she tilted her chin and walked around him.

She did not get far. A big arm shot out and stopped her.

'Quite the madam, aren't you? *I said the stairs could be unsafe.*'

'What's that to you? Any accident would be on my property. I wouldn't be coming to you for compensation.'

'No, but you'd still be a damn nuisance. We've only one doctor in the district – Helen here – also no hospital. Someone would have to look after you, and we don't go in for such handy souls.'

'I haven't been hurt yet.' She pulled away.

'No, and by heaven you're not going to be.' He pulled her back.

Helen Kemp's 'Oh, really, you two!' doused the flare between them.

Deliberately Nat went and took an old poker from beside the fireplace and probed at the narrow flight of stairs. The third rise gave way at once to the small blow.

'Your turn, Miss Milford.' He offered Peta the poker with a bow.

'I'm sorry.' She had to find the grace to say that. She added pointedly, 'But there are other methods of approach.'

'I believe we've discussed approach before.' He lit his rolled cigarette. The little ignition made a sharp punctuation in the silence that had followed after he had stopped speaking.

54

When the small noise, too, stopped, Peta held her breath as she found herself listening . . . listening to the wind finding cracks where it could enter and stir up the dust . . . listening, she thought, to the dying bones of an old house. And not such an old house as a hopeless house . . . hopeless, anyway, until she could fix it up, and that took time and money, and she had neither.

Unaware of the movement, she made a little hunch of despair. The hand on her shoulder was instant and warm. She could feel the warmth through the stuff of her blouse, and she turned. Helen? No, it was not a woman's grasp. Surely not Nat Trentham's? She saw that it was. But could this be the same man whose narrowed eyes had challenged her a moment ago? Challenged . . . and won?

There was nothing of the winner there now in the eyes, narrowed no longer, there was a concern and . . . yes, it was true . . . actually a gentleness.

'Cheese is for eating,' he acclaimed, 'but chalk is to write a message.'

'Are you trying to cheer me up?'

'I'm trying to tell you not to be a damn fool. The place is bad, yes, but it's not impossible.'

'If you have possible money, perhaps. I haven't.'

'I admit it needs attention, but it doesn't need such a deep purse.'

'My purse is shallow. Oh, can't you understand?' She shrugged the hand away. 'There would have been enough, only Uncle Claud – died. Dying is very expensive.' She was not aware that her voice had risen near-hysterically until he said softly but authoritatively, 'Drop it, Miss Milford.'

'Drop it?'

'The post-mortems. Death is expensive everywhere. You're not unique.'

'No,' . . . in anger . . . 'but this place is. Look at it! A ruin! Yet Uncle Claud paid—'

'He paid a reasonable sum. Not a bargain, I'll admit, but reasonable. Good heavens, girl, you're in another country now, a country just now in the exciting wave of prosperity, dig a hole and you find something, start something

55

and you prosper. It's our turn this century. Who knows who will be chosen next? But while a wave is rolling there are no bargains. See?'

'You can repeat that,' said Peta, looking disgustedly around once more.

He ignored her. 'You've had a bad trot, I'll concede you that. But all the same had Claud Milford been spared to come here he would have been the last to complain that he'd been taken for a fool. The place has its possibilities. Even this room ...' He stopped at that and looked around, too.

After a moment, a hard resentful moment, Peta looked around, but this time with him. At first she saw what she had seen before ... dust, plaster snow, disrepair. Disenchantment. Then she looked again. And in the silence ... Nat Trentham not speaking now, Helen Kemp just waiting, watching ... Peta felt the house breathe, not die. She sensed a fire in the dusty grate, chairs drawn up, coffee keeping hot ... It was an odd sensation, but it was *there*.

Laconically Nat broke in: 'That's enough. Don't dream any further.'

So he had read her again! Resenting his perspicacity, she flung, 'Why shouldn't I?'

'Because—' But he looked away and did not finish. He, who had warned her to go no further, now went no further himself. It puzzled Peta. She found she wanted to probe. But, with the barest touch under her elbow, another touch under Helen's elbow, he closed the subject with, 'Let's consider the rest in the car.'

From somewhere in the 'rover Helen produced a flask of coffee and poured it. The car trapped the sun and cut the winter air, and, sipping the steaming coffee, they regarded and discussed the house.

'Floor boards are surpassable,' Nat advised. 'Windows are only a minor cost.'

'What about furnishings? Floor coverings? Blinds?' broke in Peta.

'Well, you weren't expecting them, anyway.'

'No, but – well—'

'The way I see it,' he proffered, 'you must have something

56

at least in hard cash.'

'Very little.'

'Something,' he ignored, 'to start the ball rolling.'

'It would be a very slow pace.'

'It doesn't have to be done overnight. It's your stock that really matters, and this will cheer you. The barns' – he waved his arm to the huddle of outhouses – 'are in fair, if unattractive, condition. You could move right in.'

'Yes, that is good ... but it still isn't so good for me, is it? Oh, I don't mind sleeping in a barn, but—'

'Don't be a fool!' he cut in sharply.

'Where else, then?' She was angry at that 'fool' he had flung at her. 'I can't afford an inn.'

'There's none here, anyway.'

'And I trust,' she continued, ignoring his interruption, 'that you're not going to make a "fool" proposition that I can put in more nights at Goa.'

'Not after this morning's scene,' he answered promptly, 'but I do think, don't I, Helen,' ... he glanced at the doctor ... 'that *you* have something to say?'

'I've been trying to insert it for hours.' Helen's voice was plaintive. 'Peta, of course, comes back with me.'

'With you?' Peta stared at Helen Kemp.

'Why not?'

'I want no charity.'

'It would be no charity.'

'But I'm no nurse, no receptionist, I mean—'

'Miss Milford means,' put in Nat blandly, 'that it would be unspeakable for her to be employed other than in a saddle. Oh, yes, Miss Milford, Mr. Milford invariably included that ... proudly ... in his talks with me. You would be flattered indeed if you knew how frequently you, and your riding, monopolized the conversation.'

'Nat, stop it!' Helen had seen the pinched expression on Peta's face at the inclusion of Uncle Claud in the discussion. 'It's not a nurse and it's not a receptionist or anything of the sort I require' ... she had turned now to Peta ... 'it's ... well, frankly it's a third.'

'A third?'

57

'In the house. My house. At present there's only – Hansel. And – well—' a thoughtful pause – 'there should be, and must be, one more.'

'I don't understand.'

'Neither do I, really, but Hansel does. He came to me last week ... I told you, Nat ... and said, "Miss Kemp, it's not right, and until Gretel arrives there must be another one here.'

'Hansel and Gretel,' said Peta, 'it sounds like a fairytale.'

'It isn't.' Helen's voice was a little wary. 'Hansel is really Stas, for Stanislas,' she related, 'and he comes from a country that has been deprived .. yes, Peta, a migrant, and I won't tell you the details of deprivation. It's the old story.'

'But *Hansel*?' Peta was puzzled at the name; it had not the origin of a country of deprivation.

'There was little, if any, communication between us at first,' explained Helen, 'Stas's English was so new and disjointed. Then one day he happened to pick up a book of fairytales that he had grown up with the same as I had, and we "met" ' – a smile – 'for the first time really over Hansel and Gretel. After that I got to calling him Hans and he got to answering to it.'

'And Gretel? You?'

'Oh, no.' Helen shrugged that off at once. 'Gretel has some other name, but I suppose because it was unusual to my tongue, or perhaps even to create a duo, I adopted Gretel for her instead. Hans followed suit.'

'Then couldn't this Gretel be the necessary third?'

'She's not out here – yet.'

'She is coming?'

A pause, then: 'Yes.'

'But why,' asked Peta puzzled, 'am I – or any third ... all at once required like this?'

'Because all at once,' said Helen patiently, 'Hansel – Stas – is living in the town instead of at Nat's Goa. He was with Nat before, assisting in the stables, but – well, you go on from there, Nat.'

'It was not his work,' related Nat promptly, 'I saw that

58

immediately, even though I had never had better service from any hired man. I knew it. He knew it. He never complained, though, and only that I noticed how he came to life when any of the horses were sick—'

'A veterinary surgeon in the making?' deduced Peta.

'Cut out the veterinary,' said Helen quietly. 'Hansel is a born doctor, and you can take the word of a doctor not born to it.' She paused. 'Yet a doctor, for all her laboured history of patient plodding, still sharply aware of what goes to make a dedicated ... and undoubtedly brilliant ... man.'

'Please explain more,' begged Peta.

'Hansel had begun training in his own country. Because of his country's position he had to give it up. In the new régime there were no openings for careers, there were only menial jobs. But he managed to leave his country, for which' – a shrug that somehow was not so indifferent as Helen tried to convey – 'he has assured me he has only his Gretel to thank.'

'And does he?'

'I should say continually.' Helen's voice was terse.

'When Hansel came to Tasmania,' she resumed, 'he was too tired and dispirited to start his career again. But' – a smile so radiant that Peta could not miss its direction at Nat – 'someone changed that spirit.'

'I was a fool,' admitted Nat ruefully, 'I had a grand worker, a worker in a thousand, but I wouldn't let it rest at that. No, I moved Hansel into Helen's, into Berribee.'

'Where he has been accepted,' took up Helen in her turn, 'Berribee being like that. And then' – a gesture – 'he comes to me with this thing.'

'That there must be another person there?'

'Yes.'

'You should feel flattered.'

'Because – Gretel would object?' Helen came back. She laughed ... but rather a short, unamused laugh. 'Seriously, though,' she said, 'he's terribly earnest about it, so I *do* want someone. Could you and would you, Peta?'

'I can't pay you much,' demurred Peta.

'By rights I should be paying you, but if you want to be

hard to get on with you can contribute for your food.'

Peta considered a moment. 'It would help me to look around, estimate,' she agreed. 'But how would I get out here each day?'

'That fits in, too. Hansel still works at Goa for Nat ... he studies at the surgery and with my books at night. – Yes, I suppose you could say he was a kind of protégé of mine.'

'So,' put in Nat, 'you could come out with Hans each morning, go back with him at night. Well' – a little impatiently – 'what do you say?'

'What can I say except that you're terribly kind, Helen.'

'Wait till you see what I have to offer in creature comfort. It's no Goa.'

'Well, neither is Garo.' Peta's voice was rueful once again.

'Anyway,' proposed Helen briskly, 'we'll try it out at least. Unless' – an amused glance – 'you're settled where you are?'

'Here?'

'I was thinking of – Goa.'

'And *I* think,' stated Peta firmly, 'that you can put me down also as a Hansel there, for I too prefer a third.'

'Swinging England,' inserted Nat with a mock cynicism that was evidently supposed to amuse but succeeded in nettling Peta. 'Right you are, girls, we'll push back to Helen's car and Miss Milford can pick up her things. Tomorrow, or later in the week if you feel like a spell first, Miss Milford, you can begin coming out each day with Hans.'

'What about Omar and Bess and Fancy?' asked Peta.

'They don't appear to be missing you inordinately, nor do they seem to have taken a violent dislike to me.'

'You're too kind. You both are too kind,' Peta offered with tears not far from her voice.

'Well, I'm gaining,' said Helen matter-of-factly. 'I don't know about you, Nat.'

'I don't know, either. Ask me later.' Nat started the 'rover.

They did not waste time at Goa, they picked up Peta's bags and put them in Helen's small runabout, then the girls started off at once.

The countryside into the village followed the same charming tanglewood and box-thorn pattern of the track between Goa and Garo. Barribee, Peta found, was set in a small bypass from the Murchison Highway, backed again by the pansy hills, and featuring quite a surprising number of churches for such a small place all with their spires pointing to heaven. – 'Tasmania is ecclesiastically-minded,' Helen informed her, 'churches are numerous and well attended.' There were small, rather English cottages with near-English gardens with English flowers . . . hollyhocks, foxgloves and daisies.

'It's lovely,' proffered Peta.

'I think so. It's left behind in lots of ways . . . all Tasmania is . . . but there lies its charm.' She pulled up. 'This is me – Lavender House. Yes, there *is* lavender. Take a breath when you get out. Lavender does well down here. It's even harvested up at Lilydale. You must go there one day.'

'If it smells like this, I can't miss it.' Peta was out of the car now and inhaling ecstatically.

'It's the very breath of heaven.' Helen led the way down a path to the cottage, old weathered stone, but with the air that someone took pride in it, especially the scrollwork here and there that the house wore like pieces of antique jewellery.

'The surgery is to the left, a brick addition, very hygienic, very functional. Not' – added Helen with pride – 'that all my house isn't that as well, especially since Hans came. He has a well-ordered mind and likes everything to work as it was intended.'

'Will I be putting you out staying here?'

'I told you, Peta, I need someone. Or' – a short laugh – 'Hansel says so. Though undoubtedly it's his Gretel speaking.' A shrug.

'But apart from the third you now find you must have,' persisted Peta, 'won't I be a nuisance?'

'You will if you keep on as you are now. Here's the spare room. I hope it'll do.' Helen held back the door on a pleasant, sunny little corner. 'Small,' she indicated, 'but it'll only be in use at night, for I expect you'll be going out to Garo every day.'

'Also,' said Peta, 'I will only be here briefly. I simply must get started. Thank you, Helen. It's perfect.'

'Then I'll leave you to hang up your things. When Hans comes in he can carry in your heavier bags. The kitchen is to the left. We eat there. It's big and warm and the kettle is always ready for a cuppa. Come as soon as you want one, Peta, you'll find me there.'

'Thank you, I'll be right along.'

As Helen closed the door, Peta deposited her smaller bag on the bed and looked around. It was a simple room, but charming in its simplicity. The floor was bare but glowingly stained and there was a red rag mat to defeat the cold. The walls were a warm cream. For the rest, it was just a room, pleasant but nothing particular to arrest the attention. Except—

Curiously Peta crossed to the framed words on the wall. It was not a commercially printed text, it had been done by hand, and done very capably. Peta looked at the scrolls and curlicues and decorations and thought idly: I have seen writing like this before. At school? she wondered. In art class? In art books I've leafed over at the library? Then the words pushed back her leisurely conjectures and she was reading them, fascinated, instead.

For they were Peter's words. Peter's 'Drummer' words.

'If a man does not keep pace with his companions perhaps it is because he hears a different drummer. Let him step to the tune which he hears.'

Odd to read it now, she thought, remembering hearing it first on Peter's long sensitive lips.

Then she recalled that small sharp silence when she had retorted to Nat Trentham over lunch that a man can walk to a different song . . . that angry challenge from Nat Trentham when she had followed him into the yard later and he had demanded quite furiously, 'Why in hell did you have to say that?' She had pretended she had not understood him . . . but she had. Why had he attacked her about these words like that?

Still standing in conjecture, a voice reached her across the room, and she realized that the man waiting at the door must have knocked and she had not heard.

He was not at all as she had expected him, this Hansel ... Stas ... though actually she had not thought much about him at all, only listened to Helen's story.

But she would think about him now. He was the sort of man you would think about.

Across the room he smiled at her, a large, fair, rather boyish fellow with an engaging grin and soft, shy yet eager eyes.

'Miss Milford,' he said in the correct clipped syllables of the European migrant not yet up to the stage of getting his tongue with ease around unaccustomed words. 'I am Stanislas ... or Stas ... or Hansel. It is as you please.'

He bowed.

'Hansel,' chose Peta, and, crossing, she put out her hand. His own grasp was firm and warm.

'Helen has sent me,' he said, rounding each syllable carefully, 'tea is poured.'

She followed him down a rather dark passage to a big bright kitchen, a kitchen after her own heart ... and surely many hearts; Aunt Alice had had such a kitchen, her mother and her mother's friends had had them ... spacious, enough room to express oneself, cupboards galore, accommodating shelves, and, in the centre of the room, a large table for working or eating, with chairs drawn up in friendly anticipation.

On one of the chairs sat Helen, presiding over a huge brown teapot. She waved to the other chairs, and Hansel seated Peta.

'Welcome to the heart of the house, Peta,' greeted Helen, 'for that's what a kitchen is, isn't it?'

'Yes,' agreed Peta, 'and especially with a table to push your legs under, not a bar.'

'I must confess' ... Helen was pouring the tea from the big pot ... 'that I never used the table before Hans came. I stood at the sink and ate in a very inelegant hurry.'

'She was thin. She was bones and skin,' put in Hansel.

63

'We say skin and bones,' corrected Helen.

'Is bones and skin wrong, then?'

'No, not wrong, but—' Helen's eyes met Peta's eyes and they both laughed.

'It is difficult,' apologized Hans.

'I think you are doing very well,' commended Peta.

'And will do better still with you to chatter to him. Yes, Peta, I insist you open the floodgates with Hans.'

'If it is practice Hans needs surely it should be Hans opening floodgates to me,' said Peta.

'Flood? There is a flood? Gates? Where are these gates?' frowned Hansel, and, leaning impulsively across, Helen touched him companionably . . . even gently.

'There, Hansel, we say odd things again, but I do believe they are beoming less and less odd to you each day. And with Peta to talk to you the oddness will diminish further.' To Peta now: 'Yes, you're right, of course, you must both chatter.'

'The chattering brook,' said Hans proudly, 'the babbling teeth. Ah' – with a comical expression – 'I see by your faces I am wrong once more.'

'To appreciate Hansel,' said Helen after their laughter had stopped, 'you must realize that when he first came to Tasmania he had only "Yes" . . . "No" . . . "Good morning" . . . "Goodnight".'

'Tucker,' added Hans to the list with pride, 'which did for all food for me, so was very handy.'

'And handy,' Helen reminded him with a giggle, 'in your first case. No, not a case actually, Peta, but one evening when I was late a patient came and Hans was able to suggest something for the complaint.'

'He was "off his tucker",' beamed Hans, 'so I knew what to tell.'

Now they all giggled.

'I will not be able to converse medically with Hans,' demurred Peta. 'I wouldn't know how.'

'Hans just needs to be talked to, and to talk back. He must get his English much more fluent and much more extensive before he can begin his University courses. Meanwhile he studies in my office every morning before he leaves for his work with Nat, every afternoon when he returns. Every night. In his spare time' – another laugh – 'he keeps every mechanism in the house working to perfection. Oh, I tell you it was a lucky day when Stanislas from all Australia chose Tasmania.'

'Why did you?' asked Peta, who by now had gathered that these migrants could choose whichever Down Under corner they desired for their new life.

'It was unthinkable to me to wish any other,' submitted Hans. 'I had come from a small country like this, very much a terrain like this. Green hills. Green pastures. Valleys with' – carefully – 'babbling brooks. Right?'

'Right,' both girls answered at once.

'Some . . . indeed most . . . went for hot sun. I went for home. But you must not mistake me, this is now my home. And when Gretel comes—'

'But that is not her real name, Hans?' asked Peta.

'No. It is Elisabeta, but' – with loving eyes – 'of course I did not call her that.'

'Of course,' Helen's voice was a little sharp. 'And you would not be nationally peculiar there, my friend.'

'What?' he puzzled.

'It is universal, that dearest, liebe, chérie, carissima, what will you.' Helen spoke to herself, almost *at* herself. 'Elisabeta became Gretel to fit with Hansel.' Now she was addressing Peta, and her expression was enigmatical. 'I first met Stas over a fairytale, as I told you. It was at Nat's, and the tale we both knew was Hansel and Gretel. In some absurd way or other, probably because Stanislas was just too much, I called him Hansel instead.'

'And Elisabeta?' asked Peta.

'Gretel went with Hansel.' Once again Helen's voice was short.

'When will Hans be ready for university, Helen?' diverted Peta.

'When he can pass the English test. Meanwhile Nat is still employing him from half past eight to five. You will need to be ready to leave daily by eight o'clock, Peta. Will that do you?'

'Yes. You are very kind.'

After the tea Peta wandered round the garden, delighting in the fact that though it was winter even here in the south the dark season still appeared to touch hands with spring, so that the plots were never really bare. It was sharp, though, and her cheeks were apple red when she came indoors.

Hans and Helen were preparing the evening meal between them, and Peta hurried forward, insisting that while she stopped at Lavender House this, and other duties, must be allotted to her.

'No,' said Hansel definitely, 'I have so much that I owe and wish to repay.'

'And I,' put in Helen, 'just happen to like being in a kitchen. A very disappointing statement for a doctor, I know, but I'm happiest messing around with pots and pans.'

'And why is it disappointing?' asked Hans gravely. 'A woman is queen of her home.'

'Will Gretel be queen?' asked Helen rather abruptly.

'If I can make a place for her, yes, indeed.'

There was a little silence. Then Helen put down what she was doing.

'You can go ahead, Peta,' she tossed rather shortly, 'but don't think you have to do it every night, for when the work gets harder at Garo you'll feel more like flopping on the bed.'

'Hans?' demurred Peta, not wanting to give him the extra work she felt she would entail.

'You heard the man. He has to show gratitude.' A pause. 'Or is it that he really takes notes for his Gretel? Australian life must be very different in lots of ways. Are you doing that, Hans? Writing to Elisabeta as to how we deal with our vegetables, work with our meat?'

'I write to her, yes.' Hans' voice was quite calm.

'And give her advice for when she is queen?' For some reason Helen still persisted.

'Yes, Helen, that is so.'

Peta intervened a little uncomfortably, 'We can manage

now, Helen.'

'If you manage together and chatter about it as you do it, I think it will do Hans more good than an hour on his textbooks.' Helen hesitated a moment, said, 'I'm sorry I was tindery, lately I've had a little man on my shoulder, or so Nat tells me,' then turned away.

'A man on her shoulder?' puzzled Hans after the doctor had gone.

'She means a chip.'

'Ah, that I do know, it is a French-fried. Now you are laughing at me again! And yet am I not right?'

'Quite right. Look, Hans, I think we will keep to direct things first in our conversation, graduate later. – It was a nice day today, did you find it so?'

'Yes, it was very nice today,' responded Hans, 'and tomorrow it will be a nice day, also.'

'Do you think the good weather will continue next week?'

'Yes. I do not think it will rain.'

Peta answered that statement, started another channel, but kept away from the intricacies of the little man on Helen's shoulder. Or so Nat had declared.

How many things in Helen's life, she wondered suddenly, remembering that 'understanding', did Nat Trentham declare?

After dinner, Helen took surgery. Hans pored over his books. Apart from the opening and shutting of doors as patients came and went, the less than sound in the big house as Helen diagnosed and advised, the place was silent.

In her bedroom . . . a crackling fire there now, Hans must have seen to that . . . Peta unpacked her bags, or at least what she would need, then went and stood at the window for a while.

It was a glorious night, the stars cut out with silver scissors, the moon a sharp cameo. The English trees that did so well here were stripped and bare at present, but the eucalyptuses that never fell but only tattered their barks were thick with frondage, and it looked as though a frost was

67

already spreading its icing on each leaf.

Peta turned back to the warm room with its crackling fire and red rag mat. – And its framed and decorated words. '. . . Perhaps he hears a different drummer . . . let him step to the tune which he hears . . .' Peter's words. Peter, blue-eyed, dreaming-eyed Peter, Peter looking down at her and seeing the love she had for him. Oh, Peter, Peter darling! Two tears started down Peta's cheeks. She settled the fire and went quickly to bed. And there she cried and afterwards slept.

It was better in the morning, she found she could face things more ably with her emotions released and a fresh mind and heart. No, never another heart. Peter had her only heart.

However, she got up briskly, put on the slacks and heavy pullover she had left out last night, and was in the kitchen before Hans had time to ladle out the porridge. Helen came soon after, a long red dressing-gown over her pyjamas.

'Today's calls,' she yawned, 'are in a different direction from Garo and Goa, otherwise I'd call on each of you. But I'll see you both tonight.'

They left promptly at eight, doubling up the road that Helen had driven over yesterday, but different, as with all country tracks, in its reverse direction, different aspects, different shapes of trees, and now, under a heavy frost that Hans informed her would last for hours, silver-different instead of gold.

Peta asked questions about the landscape and Hans answered them slowly and laboriously . . . often, though Peta managed to keep her mouth straight, hilariously. After twenty minutes of this they both started laughing.

'We are talking in double Dutch,' Hans said proudly. 'The first time Helen said that I thought to myself: This place is British, and English is what we should speak, not Dutch. But now that is another thing I know.'

'I think you've done wonderfully.'

'I have a wonderful teacher.'

'And you will teach Gretel?'

'Yes,' Hans said. He turned off the road into the narrow

68

track that led to Garo, the hawthorns almost touching the car as it wound round the wheel indentations. 'What happens,' shuddered Peta, 'if something is coming?'

'Something is,' said Hans, listening, 'though it's not a vehicle, I think ...' Nevertheless he stopped the car and got ready to back out into the road again.

But a voice shouted through the thicket to come right through, that there was no obstacle to stop them. It sounded like Nat Trentham's voice, and when they reached the house clearing Peta saw that Nat it was. Not only Nat but several other men. Several cars and trucks. The men were already at work on the old stables ... there were ladders in evidence ... and one of the boys was making a bonfire of the discarded wood. Her horses, too, had been transferred from Goa and put in a cropping paddock. She saw Fancy trying out Tasmanian grass and apparently liking it, and knew that Bess and Omar would be somewhere around.

Hans beamed, 'You are very quick, Nat.'

'The quick brown fox jumped over the fence.' Nat was rolling his eternal cigarette and waiting for Peta's applause as well. . . or she assumed it was applause he awaited.

'A fox?' Hans looked around with interest.

'The fox must have had a long walk after he jumped the fence,' Peta said coldly. 'How many miles between us again?'

'But he is the quick fox, remember.' Nat was licking the edges of the paper together now, moulding the cigarette.

'Exceedingly quick. What' – she found she had to be critical – 'made you think I'd want the outhouses attended to first?'

'Of course you'd want them first. Don't be a fool. What goes into them is your living.'

'And what goes into the house is me.'

'Are you uncomfortable then at Helen's?'

'Oh, no, but—'

She knew he was right. And she really wanted it the way he had done it. She wanted Omar and Bess and Fancy stabled comfortably here. She wanted things got ready for the next batch to come. But the calm manner in which he had taken over things again irritated her. How did he know, anyway, if she had any money to pay these men?

'You'll be all right,' he said briefly, and she knew he had read her uneasiness, just as he had read her thoughts ever since they had met. What was it about this wretched man that he could read her so unerringly?

'Only *I* would know that,' she answered aloofly.

'Not necessarily.'

She frowned a moment, then said, 'If you mean you're intending to advance me a loan, and it must be that, for if you know as much as you say you do, you must know my assets are practically nil, then thank you, no.'

'I wasn't,' he assured her, 'I was very aware that you'd turn that down even had it been in my mind, which it was not, but I knew at least you would have the common sense *not* to turn down a business transaction.'

'Business?' she queried.

'Horse business. In which case, realizing you have no time to fritter, and knowing that these men were temporarily between jobs, I employed them on your behalf on the proceeds of that business transaction.'

'You what? And what horse business could I have at this early stage?'

'Omar, Miss Milford. Omar from High Cry and Green City. Am I right there? I have a pretty good breeding memory generally.'

'Yes, you're right.' She was staring belligerently at him.

Unabashed by her unfriendly regard, he said, 'I was never as keen about Great Harry for Colleen as I said. So—'

'So, Mr. Trentham?'

'Seven hundred dollars, Miss Milford.' He made an offering gesture with his long capable hands. 'Three hundred and fifty pounds. It's not the highest service fee by any means, but after all—'

'You mean – you mean you're actually offering to pay me—'

'That's it,' he said a little impatiently. 'It's poor for Kinrow, I know ... your uncle in one of our conversations told me that one of his fees at one time reached—'

'Yes,' Peta cut him short, 'but that was there and this is here. We've just arrived. No one knows about Omar.'

'I do.'

'You don't know whether the climate will favour him.'

'That's why you're only getting half the fee that I would have offered you at Kinrow. – By the way, did you intend changing the name from Garo to Kinrow?'

'You're changing the subject.'

'I've finished with it.

'Well, I haven't.'

'No?' he drawled.

'No!' she flung.

'What is it?' He was exhaling now ... like everything he did he did it deliberately. 'Are you taking out your dislike of me on the mare?'

'Don't be ridiculous!'

'Well, it seems like that by your attitude.'

'It's – it's your highhandedness. You announce this business, then change the subject because you're done with it. I repeat I am not done.'

'Then you'd better be, Miss Milford. And you'd better agree quick-smart. How otherwise will you pay these workers? Oh, I'm aware there will be something coming to you from your uncle, that even after death duties there must be some money, but that will take months ... could be a year ... and you have to live, or at least the stud has to.'

'I'm glad you've made a correction and cut me out!'

'I rather thought you would feel like that. I rather thought, as I do, you would always put an animal first. Look' – irritably – 'anyone would think I'd done you a disservice.'

'When all the time,' she said frigidly, 'on behalf of Colleen you are only requesting a service.' A long pause. 'It's simply that – well, I would like to do some of my own arranging for a change.'

'And what happens to your stock while you arrange? Have sense, girl, something has to begin, and begin at once. So this is it.'

He was right, and she knew it. She knew she should be

grateful, and that she should admit it. But she found it very hard.

'Thank you,' she said stiffly, 'I'll give it some thought.'

'Too late.' His eyes behind the cigarette weave were narrowed.

'For the men, yes, they are already at work, but as regards Omar—'

'Too late,' he drawled again, and, whirling around, Peta ran down to the cropping paddock, knowing before she got there that there would be only two of the three present, and that the missing third would be the big stallion.

'You're an overbearing, dictatorial, domineering interferer in other people's business!' Peta had raced back at him. 'Do you always ride roughshod over everyone like this?'

'Trust a Milford,' he commented, 'to add the horsey touch. No, I don't ride roughshod and I'm not riding roughshod now.'

'Omar—'

'Is cutting capers with Great Harry back at Goa. At least he was when I left.'

'But you said – you told me—'

'Of course I said it, but I didn't mean it. Good lord, boy meets girl before boy falls in love with girl. Don't you ever read romantic fiction, Miss Milford?'

'The third stage,' she reminded him, still angry, 'is boy falls out with girl.'

'After which the *real* thing happens for both of them. I'm glad you're not so romantically unread after all.'

'We were speaking about Omar.'

'About the animal kingdom and not ours, though I must say that of the two—'

'Spare me your views, Mr. Trentham.'

'Why should I? You didn't spare me yours. What was it? Overbearing, dictatorial, domineering—'

'You needled me,' she defended herself.

'If I did it was because you, Miss Milford, have done nothing but that to me since the first moment we met.'

'*Encountered*.'

'I'm corrected. Encountered.'

'It was when you were trespassing,' she persisted, 'in a Kinrow stable.'

'Then you later at Goa.'

'I didn't know it was yours.'

'All right.' He shrugged almost indifferently. 'It's over.'

'But Omar isn't.'

'I've told you Omar is back there with Great Harry. I didn't bring the fellow over with Bess and Fancy. For one reason I knew there wouldn't be sufficient room for all of them for several days yet. The other reason—'

'You've told me that reason already.'

'Yes, I have.' A pause. 'Well?' he inquired at last, and began reaching for his makings again.

'You said' ... her lip was trembling now and she had to turn so he would not see it ... 'that it was too late. Why did you have to be hateful like that?'

'Because there's something about you that makes me have to be positive.'

'Positively horrible!'

'Well, better that than—' He stopped.

'What, Mr. Trentham?'

'Omar simply has not been transferred here,' he said. 'If you want him over, even though there's no room, you can have him. On the other hand, my offer still stands.'

'Seven hundred dollars?'

'Yes.'

'Which I would be a fool not to take?'

'Yes.'

'Then I'll take it,' she said flatly.

'You needn't be so unenthusiastic,' he commented.

'You needn't have announced it the way you did.'

'It's obvious,' he shrugged, 'that we walk to different music.'

'Why,' asked Peta outright, 'was there silence when I said that yesterday?'

'Why did you say it?'

'No reason.'

73

'Then it doesn't matter,' he dismissed, and this time she allowed him his dismissal.

They discussed the stable at length. The men had started on the more possible of the existing buildings and said they could finish it sufficiently if roughly by dark.

'After that I should advise leaving the other barns for a while and give attention, instead, to your fences. There are some sticky spots down in the gully, you'd want to keep well away.'

'You mean Bess and Fancy?'

'*And* you. Ever heard of quicksands?'

'Are you serious?'

'They must exist, our road notices have warnings of them, though personally I have not encountered quicksands, only old mine shafts, which I *can* vouch for. So take care if you and that "boy" of yours leave the beaten track not to venture in too far.'

'Thank you for making advice of it and not an order.'

'Your pleasure, madam.' He gave a mock bow. 'Hans is giving me imploring looks from the car. I rode your Fancy over and towed Bess, and Hans knows I depend on him to get back to Goa. He's a conscientious fellow and feels he should be at work.' A pause. 'How do you find him?'

'Oh, splendid!' Peta's voice was warm.

'But not too splendid.' His own voice had an imperative note.

'What do you mean? – Oh, Gretel ... Elisabeta, I suppose. How absurd of you, as though I'd ...' A shrug, then: 'No, not too splendid. Will that do?'

'I didn't mean Gretel, I meant – However, that must fit – for now.'

'You're enigmatical,' she commented.

'As well as overbearing, dictatorial and domineering? That makes me quite a character!'

'Positive, anyway.' She felt she had won there at least.

She watched him stride up the hill to Hans, a mountain of a man covering the steep incline with long, firm steps, for all his largeness still affording that whipcord impression she had had at their first meeting, that sense of lean coiled strength.

She turned as he turned at the car to look back at her and pretended interest in the workers, a pretence that soon gave way to the real thing, for the two adjoining stables were coming up as good as any that Kinrow had offered.

'You must all be horsemen,' she praised of the order and reason.

'No, but our orders came from one,' the workmen smiled back. 'When Nat Trentham wants a thing done he puts it very clearly.'

'And sees he gets what he says,' nodded Peta, regarding the half finished job.

One of them shrugged, 'I wouldn't care to be on Trentham's wrong side. On the other hand if you're straight with him, he's the straightest man alive.'

'Quite a character!' Peta could not resist that. 'Positive.'

'There's nobody more positive than Nat.'

One thing Peta could not argue against were his positive orders for the boxes. Each box when finished would be a good fourteen feet by twelve feet, and would accommodate a horse very comfortably. She approved of the two-part door that one of the men was constructing, for horses greatly appreciated watching what was going on. The door, too, was a full four feet wide, something Uncle Claud had insisted upon. Narrow doorways were dangerous, he had asserted.

There seemed nothing she could advise on her own accord, so, after talking a while with the men, she went up to the house. Here was something that was entirely her domain, she thought, and though she could not see at this juncture from where the money would be coming, she could not resist making plans.

As she worked ... paper and pencil that she had not known were in her bag eagerly pounced on as idea after idea struck her ... Peta wondered how on earth she had looked at this house and known despair. Why, it was full of possibilities! Not only full of possibilities, but there were other things, unexpected things, as well. Beneath some of the junk she found surprise cupboards, she found

75

generous shelves and nooks. This place could be a house-wife's dream.

And not all the things were junk, either. Candle-sticks emerged, dingy and stained, but with care and much polish ... A grey-green jug with a highly glazed if dingy interior but a dull outside finish won her with its raised figure of Diana sitting with her hand on a stag's head.

She had anticipated heartache here, resentment that Uncle Claud had been taken for a fool. Several hours after-wards Peta realized that she had been enjoying herself. She also had filled her pages with sketches ... a wall knocked down there ... a room divided here. The old place, she felt almost excitedly, was coming to life.

So absorbed was she that at first she did not smell the workers' billies boiling ... that tantalizing tang of scorched green twigs and fragrant tea leaves. She did not hear their voices yarning instead of their saws singing, she was in a world of her own.

And into that world Nat Trentham strode, standing a moment to watch her absorption. A little shortly he said presently, 'All right, snap out of it, tools down.'

He had to say it twice before Peta emerged. She looked at him a little foolishly and said, 'I was actually hanging up drapes.'

'I see you've made sketches.' He had picked up her pad. She drew well and designed fluently, but either he was un-aware of her talent or it irritated him. Undoubtedly the second, for he said quite sharply, 'Aren't you running a bit too fast?'

'Oh, I'm aware that the stables must be done first, but—'

'The stables must be done first.' He ignored the 'but'.

'This' ... he actually tore out the sheet and crumpled it up ... 'is a waste of time. There are plenty of other things you could start.'

'Like?' She could scarcely join the builders, she thought resentfully; anyway, wasn't there some Government Act about that?

'Like—' He was stopped. But not for long. 'You could start a garden. You could rake around. You could' – in

76

inspiration – 'do a few sketches for improvements on *my* house.'

'Goa?'

'Yes. At a fee, of course.'

'You're very determined to play the gentleman bountiful on me, aren't you?'

'By no means. I simply know talent when I see it.'

'Yet you tore it up.'

'I told you, you're wasting your time.'

'And you would be wasting your money altering Goa,' she proffered honestly.

'You like it?' he said eagerly back.

'Very much.'

'I still think it needs a fresh touch. After all, it's been like it is for years.'

'So have all old places.'

'I don't mean alterations, I mean a change in drapes, coverings ... well, something. Look, I must take you to Entally.'

'What's Entally?'

'It's one of our most beautiful early colonial houses, and we have many for this small island. Though perhaps Woodleigh would be nearer, even though Entally is the one I feel *you'd* like.'

'Why is that?'

'Because Entally's first owner was an English girl with the same tastes as you.' As she raised her brows, he said, 'Horses. Mary Reibey was originally a convict lass sentenced at the age of thirteen for stealing a ride on the squire's horse.'

'I suppose she never rode again.'

'*You* don't suppose anything of the sort. *You* would have done what she did, go on from there. At one time ninety horses were raced from the Entally stables. But it's the house I'd really like you to see. Its charm is difficult to describe. I think the main appeal is the impression the visitor gains that it is still functioning as a home ... the clocks tick, there are fresh flowers in vases, beds are made.'

'Your bed was made the first night I arrived,' recalled Peta irrelevantly. 'I didn't realize it on first scrutiny, and

77

then—'

'And then?'

She flushed, then said stringently, 'You're exceedingly neat, aren't you?'

'A man must be neat somewhere. I'm not neat in my emotions.'

She glanced up at him and saw that his eyes were staging a little storm as presumably he thought back about something that still angered him. He would be a prickly customer, this Nat Trentham.

'Yes,' he repeated, 'not emotionally neat by any means, Miss Milford.' The storm left his eyes and he looked a little tauntingly now at her.

Somehow the look and the words embarrassed her. She changed the subject to Goa again.

'You wouldn't want to alter it at all ... perhaps a touch here, something there ...'

'Come with me and we'll look it over.'

'Now?'

'Why not? It's smoko. Crib. Nosebag-time – I don't know what you call it in England, but if you look out of the door you'll see the men are lunching.'

'Yes ... I sniffed the twigs and tea leaves.'

'You poor kid!' He was genuinely sympathetic. 'There's nothing more tantalizing than billy tea and nothing more saddening if you don't participate. You should have given a cooee and they would have invited you on the spot.'

'And shared their lunch with me? Oh, no!'

'Well, that's what I came about. Hans completely forgot to give you your flask and eats this morning ... oh, yes, he packed them. So I've brought them along. But no, I'm not giving them to you after all. Instead you can come back to Goa and drink a fresh brew there. No' – as she went to object – 'I don't intend boiling up gum twigs just for you, but I do intend boiling a jug instead of pouring flask tea.'

'Flask tea will do.'

'It's not going to do. Well, how long do you intend to stand in this house you so dislike?'

'Do you know what,' she smiled rather confidingly at

him, 'I don't believe I dislike it any more.'

With an unrewarding shortness he said, 'I wouldn't get too carried away if I were you.'

It was too late to say that, she thought; she *had* been carried away.

'But you're not me,' she replied.

'Oh, come along.' He seemed irritated. 'I'm hungry if you're not.'

They went back along the narrow lane between the hawthorns, over the wider road between apples, cow pastures, a sawmill or two and bush. Then they were entering Goa again ... Goa, the cheese to Garo's chalk. The table was set at the window once more, set as meticulously as that other time.

'Remember,' Nat said as Peta's eyes took in the immaculate arrangement, 'I have to be neat somewhere.'

'Oh, yes, the un-neat emotions.'

'I have one of those hearts' ... he was straightening a knife ... 'that can't be told.'

'I think, too,' she proffered coolly, 'you would have a bad temper.' At a resentful look from him she added, 'You are only dressing it up with your "heart that can't be told", actually that's merely part of the story, a very small part. Asperity and acrimony would be more like it. Irritable people frequently call moods something else.'

'You know a lot of big words,' he commented. 'Sit down, please. I'll ladle out the soup.'

'You said tea.'

'There's soup, too.'

'There was no need to make soup.'

'Hansel and I take soup. You please yourself.'

Hans had come in, glowing from work, the ends of his blond hair dark-wet from the sluice he had just had in the barn, eyeing his brimming soup bowl with healthy relish, accepting toast from the piled dish that Nat pushed over to him. The soup was beef and barley and mouth-watering. The steam rose in a tantalizing weave and wreathed enticingly to Peta.

Hans gave Peta a quick look and half rose. Only half,

79

though. At a glance from Nat he sat down again.

The men ate with gusto, taking slice after slice of the golden toast, discussing the stud as they stoked ... getting up and going to the sideboard to refill their bowls from the big tureen.

Evidently the lunch break was a simple affair. Apart from a bowl of tossed salad and a crusty yellow cheese ... and the inevitable brown teapot ... nothing else was offering. Nor was there need for anything else, admitted Peta. Ruefully. This was feast enough if one had the sense to—

She bit her lips at her bad behaviour that had only come back on *her*. She was extremely hungry ... Tasmanian air, she thought ... and even though the salad was attractive and the cheese looked a good one, they didn't fill a need.

'Only a fool won't change his mind,' Nat said to nobody and to nothing, but it only needed that.

Jumping to her feet, Peta took up a bowl and went, too, to the sideboard. Ladling in the fragrant broth, she invited, 'All right, tell me.'

'That you're not a fool?' He was leaning round from his chair and watching her.

'That I was one before.'

'Perhaps you were wise. Try the grub first.'

She came carefully back from the sideboard and put down the bowl, dropped in toast, sipped.

'I was *un*wise,' she judged solemnly. She looked at him a little uncertainly, then he smiled, and she smiled back. Hans smiled.

The talk returned to horses. Peta listened to Nat explaining Arabs and Anglo-Arabs, Cleveland Bays and Exmoors to Hans, how a black horse was black in colour with black points, but a brown horse, though near black, would have brown points.

'Roan can be strawberry, bay or blue,' she joined in, carried away with the conversation.

They discussed marking: star, stripe, blaze, snip. Legs with 'stockings' or 'socks'.

Hans was interested, but, as had been said of him before, it was not his world. Peta was aware of this as he dropped out of the talk and only she and Nat exchanged spirited arguments about age, something she was personally interested in since Fancy, not being officially recorded, and Uncle Claud never having told her, in her opinion had no precise age.

'Rot! Of course he has.'

'I know the usual milk and permanent teeth, but Fancy is past that stage,' she offered.

'Then you should be able to form an opinion by the shape of the jaw.'

She was getting a little out of her depth and mumbled something about ages never being certain.

'Always certain,' he came back, 'in man and beast.' He gave her a long, steady, estimating look, and she felt he was measuring out every day of her very moderate years.

'I must go down and see Omar,' she avoided. 'I mean' – as an afterthought – 'when I've done your dishes.'

Nat shrugged. 'Hans will put them in the machine. Come, then ... though be prepared for a change of heart. Your big chestnut has eyes now for another lady.'

Omar, indeed, had just that, and no wonder. Colleen, a lovely little light grey, would have won any sire's heart. But it was not one-sided, Colleen, cantering in the adjoining paddock, saw to it when she ran the fence dividing them that she ran with the chestnut. It was a pretty sight.

' Boy meets girl,' nodded Nat, watching with Peta. 'I don't think, Miss Milford, I'm wasting that seven hundred dollars.'

Peta watched them a while, then said, 'But *I'm* wasting time. I must get back to Garo.'

'It's afternoon and Tasmanian winter days are short. I think you'd better work here for the rest of the time.'

'Work?' she queried.

'That rejuvenation job I offered.'

'Then you were serious?'

'Of course.'

'But the house is lovely already, and I should think most satisfactory ... especially with only one man in residence.'

'I don't intend to keep it in this solo state.' His voice was quite matter-of-fact.

'Then the additional person might like to have his – or her – say.'

'Her.'

'All the more reason again that I should stand out. Women like to plan their own castles.'

'I'm offering you this assignment. Do you want it, or not?'

'I can do with all the cash I can snare,' she admitted candidly.

'Yes or no?'

'Yes,' she said, though not sure whether it was the right reply.

They went back to the house, and at once Hans and Nat left to attend to some fencing. Peta strolled from room to room, then paused in the dining-room. But for the car and landrover drawn up in the drive and visible through the window, here the century could have been the nineteenth, she thought. That mahogany mirror above the mahogany table, the grandfather clock and the oak press with the newspaper knife on it belonged to another era.

She decided that this was one room that must be left untouched, and went on to the library. Here there was a modern trend, though not a particularly successful one, but with plain white muslin instead of that heavy damask at the windows, the room should live its own life, not borrow from the room before.

It was like that all through the house ... the 1800s and then today. She was pleased to see the kitchen strictly today. She liked the functional end of a house up-to-date and manageable. She went up the stairs, avoiding the room into which she had barged that first night, and choosing a small room at the end of the corridor she turned the handle of the closed door.

It was an old nursery, and kept like that, and Peta stood enchanted. A slipper bath, a child's cradle, everything small and delicate. She smiled and came out again.

She went into another room, evidently a second, or spare, bedroom. It was entirely different from the rest of the house ... modern and artistic, but artistic in the 'arty' sense.

82

Studied, she thought, more than won. Contrived more than achieved. She stood longer in the room than the room deserved, but somehow curious about it . . . somehow feeling she had known it . . . or something about it . . . before. She went out again and down the stairs, and was standing looking at a photograph when Nat Trentham came in.

There was no one she knew in the photograph, which, of course, was not surprising. It was a family scene: a woman with two boys.

'Myself when young,' Nat tossed carelessly of the taller of the boys.

'I wouldn't have recognized you,' Peta tossed as carelessly back . . . but she wasn't looking at Nat Trentham 'when young', she was looking at the other child.

I could almost say, she told herself, I have seen him before. The woman she found she could not care much about. Pretty, admittedly, but in a meaningless kind of way.

Nat's 'What's your verdict?' set her replacing the photograph and telling him how the drawing-room and nursery must not be touched, but how the damask in the library could be dispensed with, some of the mahogany still in use in the other rooms relieved with a touch of colour here and there.

He listened to her seriously, nodding from time to time.

'How did you like the spare?' he asked when she had finished.

'I didn't, but—' She left it at that. How could she say that even in her dislike of it . . . no, not dislike really, simply lack of enthusiasm . . . she had still lingered there? She became aware that he was looking at her quite intently, and she shrugged, 'That's all, I think. When can I go?'

'You're very anxious.'

'Helen is so good having me I would like to help out all I can.'

'Then help by not helping too much. Understand? Don't cut Hans out. I said that before.'

'I'd rather gathered you meant me not to cut Gretel out,' she said coolly.

'Well, you gathered wrongly. Gretel isn't in this. She's

83

not even here. Helen is.'

'*Helen*?' She stared at him, finding it difficult to believe that this man was advising her so oddly. After all, hadn't he told her that there was an 'understanding' between himself and the doctor?

She did not comprehend, and when he made no attempt to explain himself, she said aloofly, 'Have no fears for Hans because of me. I have no interest in men.'

'Oh, come, young women of your age are always interested in men.'

'You don't know my age.' She had forgotten the estimating look, that feeling that he was measuring out every day of her years.

'Man and beast,' he reminded her succinctly. 'And I still say that young women of your age—'

'I'm not interested.'

'You are the exception, then? Yet you appear very normal to me.'

Flushed, she tossed, 'I should have said I'm not interested *in other men*. Will that do you?'

He was rolling his cigarette again, taking his time, giving it his attention and making everything else wait.

Not that there was anything to wait for, and she turned to the door through which she could see Hans standing by the car ready to go into Berribee.

'No, Miss Milford,' his voice came cool, clipped and very surprising, 'it will not do. Goodbye for now. Tomorrow don't let Hansel forget to hand you out your lunch.' He followed to add as she ran down the steps: 'Also the flask.'

CHAPTER FOUR

PETA had no intention of letting Hansel forget because she had no intention of repeating the day's performance, of putting herself in the way of Nat Trentham's charity a second time. From now on it would be a flask and a sandwich for her.

But when she awoke on the second morning at Lavender House she could see, unless she worked strictly indoors, that it would be useless travelling out to Garo. For it was pouring with rain.

At least that was what Peta called it, but Helen laughed at her at breakfast and corrected, 'New-chum, it's only a Scotch mist, Tasmanian variety.'

'You call that a mist!' Peta looked at the fat drops coursing down the windowpane.

'Compared to the rains up north, it is. Oh, I suppose you find it rather decided, but the Aussie mainlander over here would dismiss it as a drop of dew. It really rains up there. All the anvils ring at once. Five minutes afterwards there is shining sun.'

'You would mean on the coast, I suppose?'

'And the inland.'

'I thought that would be a rainless desert.'

'It is a desert, and often rainless, but when the rains come, and believe me they do come, they cram everything into a couple of hours. Where you never suspected even a creek, a river, miles wide, will suddenly appear. In no time you have an inland sea. And that desert of yours, Peta, becomes a garden, flowers you have never dreamed of, every shape, every hue.'

'It sounds fascinating.'

'It's strange and rather wonderful.' Helen's eyes dreamed a little.

'You've visited it?'

'No.'

'Then—?'

'I was born there.'

'In the desert.'

'The flowering desert.' Helen reminded her proudly, 'that is' ... truthfully ... 'at times. But I didn't see as much of it as you might imagine from my home airs. Instead of School of the Air, or Correspondence, as most inland children are given, I was sent down to boarding college. There were only the vacations, and more often than not my parents preferred to get away and we went to some

85

beach, for me to get to know my home town.'

'But since then——?'

'I haven't gone back. My father died my second year in training ... my mother soon afterwards. You have to have something to pul you back, haven't you?'

'Do you want to now?'

'Oh, no, it finished for me with them. But I always think of it with wonder. I tell Nat he must go up and try a race there.'

'A race?'

'The Inside ... it's called that more than the Inland .. Races are fantastic.'

'But Mr. Trentham is not interested in that part of his business.'

'I believe he could be. After all, what's the use of breeding a blue blood and not enjoying the real thrill? One of those picnic races could be a forerunner to a Melbourne Cup, who knows? At least it would be an experience he would never forget.'

'I believe you're wistful,' suggested Peta.

'No, I put that behind me when I came down here.' Helen sounded quite matter-of-fact.

'What a contrast,' commented Peta, looking out of the window where the rain was forming silver runnels in the garden. 'Here is no desert land. How did you chance on Berribee, Helen?'

'It was no chance.' Now Helen's voice was short. 'I came – by design. I – stayed on.' She stopped herself at that, and Peta dropped the subject ... but she could not stop her train of thought. What design? Nathaniel Trentham with whom she had an 'understanding'?

She looked at the rain again and said, 'I feel a loafer not being on the scene today, but what could I do?'

'Nothing. Anyway, Peta, you couldn't get there. On days like this it's arranged that Hans spends his time here on his studies, for there's little to do at the stud when it's wet. I suppose I could drive you to Garo, only—'

'You have your rounds,' nodded Peta.

'Only,' continued Helen with a pleased look, 'I'm going to

drive you somewhere else instead. I haven't any visits today, and that's far too precious a situation not to grab. You and I, my girl, are spinning up to Woodleigh.'

'The old colonial home.'

'You've heard of it, then?'

'Yes.' But Peta was a little dubious. She wanted to see the place, but Nat Trentham had spoken of it first, spoken of taking her there, in which case she had no doubt that those 'untidy emotions' of his (her words were quick temper) would become untidier (or quicker) still should she steal a march on him and go instead with Helen.

'You're not so keen on the idea?' Helen must have seen her indecision.

'Oh, yes, only . . . well, Mr. Trentham . . .'

'I'll fix him,' Helen shrugged airily.

'I suppose you will,' said Peta of her bland confidence. 'He told me that first day of your – understanding.'

'Nat and I are very close.' A pause. 'But just to be on the safe side with that hothead we'll change Woodleigh to Redmarley, even more convenient and equally old. There are holly trees there, will you be homesick?'

'No. You see, like you, I put all that behind.'

'You must tell me some time, Peta.' Helen's eyes were kind.

'Thank you, I would like to. Now you tell me more about Redmarley.'

'Its advertisement in the old *Advertiser* once was "a genteel residence with all the appurtenances fit for a respectable family".' They both laughed.

Hans had joined them, and he looked at each girl in confusion. 'But you laugh at gentleness. Why?'

'Genteel, not gentle,' explained Helen. 'Genteel is well-bred and elegant, but gentle is—'

'I know gentleness.' As Hans said it he looked at Helen, and Peta felt a pang for the big blond man. Surely by now he, too, must have learned of Helen's and Nat's 'understanding'?

Rather hurriedly she said, 'You don't go out to Goa today, then, Hans?'

'I work instead in Helen's office.'

'And to afford you perfect quiet, Peta and I will leave you to it. Don't take long dressing, Peta, it's not so far, but the time still gets away here in winter.'

They were on the road within the hour, and with every northern mile the sky got clearer. By the time they reached Redmarley it was a glorious morning.

When Peta pointed this out a little guiltily, Helen reminded her that they had crossed a mountain and that weather can be different each side of a mountain. Personally, though, she said, she hoped for sunshine back home as well as here, because on bright days people felt better, which meant that Hans would not be disturbed by phone calls.

There was a gentle tug to her mouth as she said it that made Peta wonder. What was the true position here? Hans spoke of Gretel but looked at Helen. Helen had an understanding with Nat but her eyes had gentleness for Hans. And where did Nat fit in?

'Is there any social life in Berribee?' Peta asked Helen.

'You mean more contemporaries than our own group, for it is that since you made a convenient fourth, isn't it? And yet isn't our group enough? We at least add up to a round figure with equal sides to each sex.' As Peta did not comment, Helen answered, 'But no, as a matter of fact there isn't. The young people all move out for jobs. And that's more often the case than not in little Apple Isle. I'm sorry, Peta, if it's restricting.'

'I didn't mean it like that. Anyway, I'm not interested.'

'All women are.'

'Perhaps,' corrected Peta honestly, 'I should have added – now.' She had answered that, too, she recalled, to Nat.

'I thought that once.' Helen's voice came quite detached. The detachment must have reached her as well, and she seemed a little surprised at herself.

She stopped at Redmarley House. The dazzling winter sunshine on the old colonial architecture brought the place vividly to life. As Peta stood in the courtyard and looked at the four-stall stable, coach house and store room she could feel the century blurring around her, see the servants coming down from their loft rooms to work in the huge flagged kitchen, to answer the bell chords connected with each room of the house.

'Grim, wasn't it,' said Helen beside her of the bells, 'and yet am I not a servant of bells myself?'

'You're going to be.' The voice cut in before Nat Trentham did. The two girls turned round in surprise, for he was the last person they had thought to see. 'I bear a message, fair lady' ... he was addressing the doctor ... 'from our good Hans. Mrs. Ferry has started pains.'

'She can't.' Helen was frowning. 'She's not ready.'

'She can.' Nat gave Helen a small edged smile. 'And that will teach you to steal a march on me,' he accused.

'A march?'

'I planned this first.' He waved his big arm to the old house.

'But you had spoken about Woodleigh. Peta said so.'

'It was still a march stolen.'

'All right then, but I'm not taking the entire blame, Peta was not exactly protesting.'

'That I can well imagine.' Now the voice was dry.

'But how is it,' Helen was asking ... Peta standing silent ... 'that you're here so soon?'

'I've a faster car than has Doctor Kemp,' he pointed out. 'I also took a less long, if rougher, road. Again the phone message came just as you went through the gate. Hans rang Goa at once, then went out to Mrs. Ferry himself.'

'But Hans can't ...' Helen was frowning even deeper.

'He has. It's a funny thing, but babies don't ask first to look at college degrees.'

Annoyed with herself, Helen said, 'I was sure about Jean. I'm still sure.'

'Then don't be too sure, and take my car. Miss Milford and I will return in your tortoise.'

'Thanks, Nat, I suppose I'd better push off.'

'But not off the road in your hurry. Promise me, Helen.'

'I promise. Sorry, Peta.'

Peta said it was all right ... which she meant most certainly for Helen if not for herself.

More 'untidiness', she was thinking, from 'untidy emotions', or, as she thought of it, more fuel for a quick temper, for certainly that pull now to Nat Trentham's long mouth did not cheer her. How autocratic, how everything his way, this man was! But his first words after Helen had disappeared round a curve in Redmarley's drive surprised her.

'All right, Miss Milford,' he advised quite mildly, 'don't trip over your lip.'

When she looked up at him she saw that the pull to his mouth had gone and he was actually grinning with amusement at her. It made a boy of him, which surprised her, he was always so much the matured man.

'It wasn't all that important looking at old things, was it?' he asked. 'Not on a new day like this. It's still early, so what do you say?'

He was unpredictable, he was a crosscurrent and a contradiction, and what Peta said was: 'I simply don't understand you.'

'If you wish to, just say the word.' Now his eyes were glinting into hers ... asking ... inviting ... challenging.

The glint dazzled her, but she pretended it was the sun and moved away. She had never met a man quite like this man.

'Put it down to the different drummer that I walk to,' he advised lazily, reaching for his makings. Once more, she resented, he had read her.

They crossed together to Helen's car and he held open the door for Peta to get in.

'We'll go home by some of the forest tracks,' he said. 'I think the tortoise is sound enough. But hold tight, Miss Milford, it's no freeway where I'll take you now.'

It certainly wasn't, but it was a wonderful experience ... if you remembered not to look down. The track from the moment they left the main road was little more than wheel-ruts ... twice it crossed a fast-running creek and climbed a precipitous and rocky gorge ... twisted between rain-forests of tall trees and dense shrubs ... quite unexpectedly came out to a deserted settlement that Nat Trentham related had been one of the mushroom towns that had sprung to life almost overnight and died even quicker than that after gold fever days over a century ago.

'This,' he recounted, 'was all gold country. Still is. All this West Coast is mineral – zinc, lead, silver, gold, and the rest. When Abel Tasman's ships edged their way round our part of the coast the compass needles fairly danced from the deposits of iron ore.'

He had pulled up the car in the ghost town and he said, 'It must have been good here in those times, it took a mining town to know how to put on a show. I can see it ... brass bands, visiting theatrical troupes, hotels fairly humming from the bonanzas of silver and the hills of nickel.

'And now it's gone.'

'Don't you believe it. It's here all right, but it's easier to get at farther down. The same rain-forests and fern gullies extend south, but they open out, so it's more convenient there for the aerial ropeways of bucket conveyors feeding the ore to the refinery. In which case timber has taken over here, instead. Listen.'

As she did so, Peta heard the whine of mechanical saws somewhere down a deep valley.

He started off again, the track still tortuous, and as they edged round hair-pin bends, descended steeply to scrape over rock bottom creeks, forced their way through encircling rain-forests that reached their branches together high above them, he told her about a bushman years ago who had axed his mate somewhere in these ramparts, but when he tried to escape, each time found himself back at the scene of the crime. 'The Track that came back,' the story was called.

'Will we find ourselves back at Ghost City?' shivered Peta.

'In several minutes we'll be on the road to Goa.'

'*Goa?* But—'

'There'll be no one at Doctor Kemp's,' he reminded her.

'I was thinking of Garo.'

'In what way?'

'Work, of course.'

'It appears you were not thinking of it earlier.'

'So there's to be a Please Explain after all.' Peta sighed and patently resigned herself.

'Yes,' he agreed seriously, 'but not in the way you expect.'

'You intrigue me.'

'Not as much as I was intrigued ... intrigued with your Bess.'

'Brilliant Bess. What about Bess?'

He did not look at her, he kept on driving, negotiating those wheel ruts between the trees. 'Have you suspected she may be having a foal?' he asked.

'Bess? Why – why, no.'

'It happens,' he reminded her.

'Yes, but—'

'Look, isn't it likely that your uncle would have planned it this way? After all, a stud functions rather with that idea.' As she sat silent, he persisted, 'Haven't you received his records yet from Kinrow, his books of data – and more particularly dates?'

'Uncle Claud was a fund of information in himself,' she returned stiffly.

'You're really saying,' he interrupted cruelly, 'that he never included you there. Oh, I know you've attended a foaling, or so you've said, but I also think you know very little actually about the whole thing. I'm not blaming you, you're not the first "pony girl" to fancy herself as a breeder by far, but good lord, woman, how do you expect to go on from there? The owner of your own stud?'

Sullenly Peta said, for that 'pony girl' had struck home: 'Bess is not in foal.'

'And how would you know? Come on, tell me that.' He flashed her a challenging look.

Awkwardly she replied, 'Well – well, she's agile, not – bulky.'

'If she were bulky it could be too much feed just as well.'

There was a silence as he manipulated the last indented ruts to join the main road again.

'I don't want to go to Goa,' Peta stated flatly.

'I have the mare there,' he informed her just as flatly.

'How dare you take her away? Why did you? The stables at Garo are quite comfortable now.'

'I felt she should be looked over.'

'But—' began Peta angrily.

'Looked over by someone who knows. See here' . . . a brief pause . . . 'I may be wrong.' But his tone said clearly that he did not think so; that *his* being wrong was entirely unlikely.

'You are,' Peta flashed.

'And how would you know?' he asked again. 'How would a pony girl know?'

Flushed, she answered, 'I'm not just a pony girl and I'm not entirely a fool, I know a little about – things at least.'

'Very little. But that's not the question I really intended. How would you know, or not know, during the period of your uncle's upheaval, *what* happened to Bess, for as far as I could see when I was there all you did was police Kinrow, remove the undesirables—'

'Including you,' she put in angrily.

'While in between' . . . he deliberately ignored her . . . 'you gazed dreamily out over paddocks.'

'They were meadows there. Anyway, how would you know?'

He copied her own words. He said, 'I'm not entirely a fool.' Then after a pause, and in a different voice: 'What caused those dreams? Some man?'

'No.'

'Oh, come, Miss Milford!' He laughed softly and tauntingly, and defensively she flung back at him:

'I hadn't met him then.'

'Oh, so there was one?'

'There is now,' she snapped, hoping that would finish it.

When he did not comment, she demanded, 'But what's this to do with Bess?'

'A whole lot, as a matter of fact. If no record of service is on your uncle's books, then I think you can put down

93

your Bess's condition to – well, to be brutally frank, your own inattentiveness.'

'I think you're abominable!'

'But, luckily for you, perspicacious. I feel almost sure the mare is going to foal.'

'Shouldn't a vet man be certain?' coldly.

'No,' wearily. 'Every sign is an indicator, but nothing is a certainty. Perhaps our lack of certainty is because the birth-rate in horses is phenomenally low. They are difficult productively.'

'And you blame *me* for being ignorant.'

'I blame you for pretending not to be.'

'But I'm not ignorant, I'm not.'

'The pony girl turned breeder,' he repeated cynically. 'Look, why not cut your losses now, even make a handsome profit? My offer to take over Garo still stands.'

'My refusal still stands. And if you don't mind I'll get off right here. Someone will be able to run me into town.'

She had expected blank refusal and was a little discountenanced when he halted at once and opened the door.

'Bus comes along in ten minutes,' he advised her. 'You needn't thank me for the ride.'

'I wasn't going to. Nor for your advice ... false advice ... on Bess.'

'Right.' He swung into gear.

'Fancy,' she called as he started to move off. 'Fancy will be by himself at Garo.' Her gregarious Fancy, she knew, would not like that.

'Isn't it rather late to think of your lack of supervision?' He had stopped the car briefly to look at her narrowly, but when she did not pick up the innuendo in his words, he said, 'Don't fret, I brought him back to Goa as well as the mare.'

'You have all three there?'

'Yes.'

'Kindly return them by tomorrow morning.'

'And you will return your seven hundred dollars?'

She looked blankly at him ... she had not thought of that.

94

'It's all right,' he shrugged after he had let her stew for a few minutes. 'I won't be demanding it. I feel confident that this time next year a little Oleen or Comar or what-do-you-suggest will be tripping our Tasmanian green grass.' He smiled in a friendly fashion, but she only stared stonily back at him. 'Well,' he shrugged, 'happy bus ride,' and this time really accelerated to leave her standing there.

Only when he had gone did she realize she had no money, that if a bus did come along as he said she would have embarrassing appeals to make of the driver. Besides, what would that driver and his passengers think of her, joining a bus in the middle of – well, in the middle of Tasmania like this, for that's what it seemed to her, just hedges on each side of the road, and behind the hedges bush.

But, fortunately for Peta, for although she had thought out an explanation it still sounded even to its composer's ears very unlikely, a car came along first. In twenty minutes she was back at Lavender House, finding the door on the latch so no trouble to get in.

She took off her coat, then made some coffee. While she was drinking it, the phone rang. It was Helen. Mrs. Ferry had been right, and she and Hans were staying with her. Would Peta put any emergency patients on to Doctor Jensen in the next town?

Helen had lost her pique at being so far out in her timing for Jean Ferry and now sounded a little breathless and excited. Well, Peta supposed, birth would be the most breathless and exciting thing in the world. Which brought her back to Brilliant Bess, who, and now Peta faced it, had never been as brilliant as her name suggested. Secretly it had puzzled her when Uncle Claud had made Bess one of his few selections to bring out to Australia, had included her in the first consignment. A pretty thing, yes. Nicely-bred, yes. But never an outstanding filly. More in Fancy's class.

What was it that man, that Trentham, had said of Fancy? – 'Isn't it rather late to think of your lack of supervision?' That sounded as though he was criticizing her attitude to Fancy. Probably doubting that she was as fond

95

of her darling grey as she implied. Well, she would show him. She would get her favourite boy back from Goa first thing tomorrow, and the two of them would ride like they used to ride in Kinrow days, race the fields until they became one unit instead of rider and horse, ride until little things like – like things to do with Nathaniel Trentham were even less than the grass barely kicked up by Fancy's nimble hooves. For there was nothing, *nothing*, like the rapport between rider and horse.

She set the table for the evening meal, but when Hans and Helen did not arrive she put the things back again, settling for just a sandwich and a glass of milk.

Finally she went to bed, but was still awake when the car came up the drive. She heard Hans and Helen in the passage, laughing softly together, Hans bursting into song to which Helen warned, 'Ssh! Peta's asleep.'

'But I'm not.' Peta leaned up in the darkness on her elbow. 'What's the news?'

'Twins – a boy and a girl. My very first. I should say *our* first.' Helen's voice trilled. 'I don't know how I could have coped without Hans. Meanwhile Jean and pair have gone up to hospital *after* the event.'

'Tomorrow,' said Peta plaintively, 'I want some maternity lessons from you two. There's a certain young lady called Brilliant Bess, and I've been advised—'

'Brilliant Bess sounds like a mare, and though we know we're brilliant' ... Helen was in high spirits ... 'that's Nat's territory. Ask him.' She yawned. 'Every man to his own trade.'

'And to the beat that he hears.' Peta could not have said why she added that except that she was staring in the direction of the now obscured text on the wall.

There was silence in the passage ... suddenly heavy silence after the light laughter.

Then Helen Kemp said quite abruptly, 'Goodnight, Peta. Goodnight, Hansel.'

Peta heard her go along to her room. Presently she heard the door close as Hans went down the stone path to his garage flat.

CHAPTER FIVE

PETA did not lose her cares the next morning in the instant manner that she had promised herself, for the car from Lavender House and the contingent from Goa Stud arrived at Garo together, and Nat Trentham had something to say.

Brilliant Bess had been returned as Peta had demanded, but any triumphant comment Peta might have made as to how even 'wise heads' sometimes make mistakes was precluded by the vet's dry: 'I would say that that inattentiveness occurred around March. Miss Milford, does March coincide with love's young dream?'

'Bess's?'

'Bess's stablehand's.' He started on his cigarette ritual. 'Fortunately for Bess, Tasmanian high summer isn't such a trial, for that's when she'll foal.'

'You're very sure of yourself.'

'As well as sure of Bess. High summer here is half a year away, so she'll be all right at Garo for at least some months.'

'She'll be all right at Garo, period.'

He looked at her narrowly. 'If it was only the mare I'd let it go at that, the trouble entailed when the time comes would be your just deserts, for heaven knows it's no picnic ever, but I happen to like horses.'

'So do I.'

'Then do you intend to stable them tonight in boxes like that?' He waved his arm to the finished work, but only finished as regards the carpenters.

'No. That is . . . I mean . . .'

'If I were you I would get cracking.' He tethered her three, got back on to his own mount . . . he had led her trio . . . and rode off.

Angry at his criticism but knowing he was right . . . was this Nat Trentham ever wrong? . . . Peta did what he had advised, she got right into work. In the narrower storage compartment at the end of the boxes she arranged saddle

97

on saddle horse, grateful that the men had found time to make her one, dismissing an unwelcome suspicion that they had been instructed to do so. By him. All her equipment was in good clean order, she had attended to it frequently on both ships, so now she found she could place, without more fuss, the girths, stirrup leathers, buckle guards.

Besides the saddle horse an all-round bench had been provided, a welcome number of hooks attached to each wall. She hung up everything ... a place for the brushes ... a place for rugs, clothes, wither pads. On one of the benches she arrayed the saddling cleaning aids and the soft rags and burnishers to deal with the cleaning. The bridles went on hooks, their buckles back to their proper places with strap ends into their keepers and runners.

A big record book took up pride of place on the small table with the stool drawn up to it, and on the bench above the table she placed her collection of manuals that she had carried with her from Kinrow. All it needed now was a calendar, there must always be a calendar, and Peta was disconcerted to find one rolled up and secured with elastic and placed on the table in readiness. Opening it out and flattening it prior to hanging it up, she saw that February next year in a little windowpane at the side of the present year was ringed in red ink. It was marked B.B. Her lip curled.

'Doctor Knowall,' she said to the completed office, and flounced along to start on the boxes.

She had done this so often it came mechanically. The mangers at breast-level, shallow enough for jaws not to be caught in them, deep enough to prevent food thrown about. The wooden bucket for watering that Uncle Claud had thought so highly of that he had never changed with the times for anything else, that he had even insisted she carry on the ship. – 'Sweet and clean,' she recalled now from dear old Uncle Claud, 'no injury to the horse and hard to knock over.' She touched the weathered wood with affection.

In the storage department she placed the barrow, shovel, broom and the stable fork with its blunted points that had travelled, like the bucket, out with her and been brought over from the mainland with the horses. She was pleased that the storage compartment was out of reach of the boxes, for injury could be done to a curious horse, and she put down this precaution once more to the Lord of Goa.

Now all that was needed was straw, and by now it was not at all surprising to Peta that she found it standing ready to be placed in the approved manner, and that was distributed evenly across the surface but piled thicker around the four walls as a guard against injury.

Now it was all done, and Peta could not help looking at it with approval. The wheat straw that had been provided gave a bright appearance to the stable as well as promised a warm and comfortable bed.

She went out to where her three were tethered and talked to them as she used to talk at Kinrow, as she had on the journey out.

'It's a crib for a king, and you must all lie down and rest sometimes, because long hours on your feet will jar them.'

Omar looked rather loftily at her, she thought, Bess abstractedly . . . was Bess thinking of something else? Something in high summer? . . . but Fancy nuzzled into her as always and Peta nuzzled back.

'All right, my darling,' she laughed, 'I promised myself something . . . you, too, because you love it as well . . . and now I'm going to do it. You and I are going to blow away cobwebs, Fancy boy.'

She carefully stabled Omar and Bess by headstall and leadrope. They were not at all unwilling, probably they were glad to settle in. Making sure they could see out . . . another of Uncle Claud's insistences . . . Peta got her saddle and came out to her best boy. As she saddled up she felt her old thrill at the thought of riding until horse and rider became one unit instead of two, until the rapport between them mattered more than anything else she knew, all over again.

Fancy must have anticipated it as well, for he gave a little whicker of pleasure. In another moment they were both free and cantering away from the stables.

Fancy took the boundary fence, that was, as Nat Trentham had said, badly in need of renewal, in his usual manner, head and neck stretched to full extent, hind legs gathered up under his belly. Peta went with him as though she was a counterpart. Almost at once the terrain dipped down, and Nat's taunt of 'chalk' compared to his own 'cheese' was proven in several marshy sections. However, if not as well-endowed as Goa, Garo was still far from impossible, for a lot could be done by drainage, and, taking Fancy over some fallen logs and making for the first foothill of the pansy blue backdrop of mountains that rose up between the two studs and the West Coast, Peta thought triumphantly that at least Garo could claim its share of beauty as well as that place next door.

For beautiful . . . as beautiful as anything she had ever seen . . . were the fern gullies that opened up to her. To left and to right glades so green that even the air seemed green-tinted met under myrtles and sassafras that grew so tall and spread such branches that the sky could only be glimpsed in blue and white snippets. But you were aware of cliffs and peaks even though you could not see them through the thick leafage, you sensed deep valleys, isolated rocks, gorges above which waterfalls splayed silver mists. Why, there was moisture now on Fancy's coat, a silver fine-ness misting the air.

She could have kept on and on, but she was not going to be a fool, it would be easy to get lost here; also Nat Trentham had spoken of quicksands, even though he had not experienced them himself, and of old mine shafts, that he had experienced. So, with a little sigh of satisfaction and a promise to Fancy as well as to herself to come again, Peta turned back.

However, Fancy, usually compatible, was oddly reluctant to turn on this occasion. His ears were pricked at some-thing, so Peta listened, too, but heard only the sough of leaves and a little noise that could have been animal or bird. Not caring to investigate for all Fancy's unwillingness to leave, she turned firmly back to Garo.

As she came up the slope again the Goa car pulled

up and Nat got out. He flicked his glance at her on Fancy, then said, 'I trust you remembered what I told you and didn't venture too far.'

'I'm here, aren't I?' she responded briefly.

'Yes. It looks like you.' All at once he gave one of his unexpected boyish smiles that, even though you did not want to be disarmed, disarmed you. 'What did you think of it down there?' he asked.

'It's glorious. It's – it's almost breathtakingly so.'

'Hard to leave,' he nodded.

'Fancy found it hard, anyway, he was all for stopping, he heard something that aroused his curiosity, I suppose. Could it be a Tasmanian Devil?' She had read about these Tasmanian Devils, only thirty inches long, ferocious, quite untameable and extinct everywhere else for many centuries yet still found here.

'Horses exhibit nervousness, not curiosity, when there's a Devil around,' declined Nat, 'they can't understand that husky cat-dog voice.'

'Then it wasn't Mr. Devil talking to him,' nodded Peta, dismounting. 'One has the feeling,' she added wonderingly, 'that anything could be there.'

'Well, if not there then certainly further down.' He was taking Fancy from her, but for a moment he stopped to turn, his eyes agleam. 'Can you imagine it in this year of grace,' he said as he had once before, 'these times of mod. cons., that terrain that literally no man has penetrated still exists. It's a wonderful and a sobering thought that this little island of ours is possibly the last wilderness.'

She nodded eagerly; she had felt that same thrall even down in the glade of ferns, so how much more impressive would it be in that untrodden south-west corner of this beautiful last island.

He had stepped into the stables and she stepped after him, anxious now, though she would not have admitted it, for his reaction. When it came after close scrutiny of each box, of the storage compartment, of the office, it was so complimentary that Peta's cheeks burned – but burned pleasurably. It was nice to be praised.

'Top marks, Miss Milford. You may be a "pony girl", but you're still a damn good strapper.'

'Thank you.'

'You really did get cracking, no daydreaming and looking over meadows this time.'

'Fields,' she corrected, but still pleased with herself.

'I can't see anything that I wouldn't have done the same way myself,' he went on.

'Then that' – a faint note of sarcasm in her voice – 'is indeed praise.'

He grinned at her acidity and said, 'I deserved that. Look, I won't reward you with words after all, I seem to have a knack of saying the wrong thing. I'll reward you with a letter instead.' He handed it across.

'Mine?' she queried.

'You sound surprised.'

'I am. How would you have it?'

'Elementary. The mailman can't come to an address that's not yet an address in actuality. So he left it with me. If you don't like the idea of my handing on your letters I would advise you to advise your correspondents to write in the future to you care of Lavender House.'

'I will. Though I didn't mean it that way, I really mean I didn't resent *you* bringing it ... is anyone ever resentful over mail? ... I just—'

He shrugged away her apology and said that he only hoped that this letter kept up the unresentful reputation, then he went on to explain that Hans was remaining at Goa for the night ... some vet matter the two of them were tackling together ... and that Miss Milford, unless she cared to stop over, too ... an inquiring look at Peta and Peta's faint cool shake of her head ... could have the car and drive herself back to the surgery.

'You do drive, I presume?'

'Yes. But how will you get back to Goa?'

'Failing you taking me, and it is a little early yet for a working woman to down tools, I expect, I thought you might offer me Omar.'

'Seven hundred dollars?' Peta could not resist that.

'I told you,' he reminded her, 'that I didn't believe any return service would be necessary. No, I'm asking for Omar because Bess is not advisable' . . . he flicked her a reminding glance . . . 'and because your own Fancy, of course, being a one-woman horse, would be out of the question.'

'Quite out of the question,' she agreed warmly.

'Omar, then?'

'I suppose so. Does Helen know Hans won't be coming home?'

'She'll know when he doesn't, just as she would know if you didn't. It's easy come at Lavender House. Are you sure you don't want to change your mind and save yourself that drive?' The bramble eyes that looked across at her were quite inscrutable.

'Sure,' she said, and began unfastening Omar for him.

'I've brought a saddle.' He took it out of the car.

When Peta led the stallion out of the box to him he had Omar ready in a flash, and was mounted as quickly. They made quite an imposing spectacle, the big man, the big horse, Omar showing off with little sidesteps and Nat Trentham allowing him to, the while he still kept a firm rein.

'Don't leave it too late tonight, Miss Milford,' he advised. 'Winter evenings come early and you're still new around here.'

He turned the horse and then, Peta watching, took a cool run and jumped the high gate, not just a broken fence, not a log, but an upstanding gate.

'Doctor Showoff Knowall,' Peta added to her name for him, and deliberately she did not raise her hand to his good-bye salute.

She went inside, sat down on the stool and opened the letter. She had seen at a quick glance that it was from Mr. Gillett and she was anxious to know the latest news.

It was not good news. Mr. Gillett, after a short preamble, got right to work, and his words considerably disturbed Peta. By this she had known not to expect too much from Uncle Claud's bequest, not after death duties had taken their share, so it was not that that dismayed her. It was Mr. Gillett's:

When I wrote telling you that you were your uncle's sole legatee but not to anticipate any fortune, I thought that was the end of the matter.

However, not being your uncle's solicitor, I only had this from Mr. Benton of Benton and Blowes, who handled Mr. Milford's affairs. So I was not in the position, not having actually read the will, only being acquainted about it from Benton, of knowing its actual terms.

My dear, when your uncle made this will he could never have thought of what was to happen to him so soon, otherwise he would not have put what money is to come to you in strict trust until you turn twenty-five.

I know this will be a blow to you, especially after you have refused my advice that you sell out at once and have already possibly incurred extra expense.

But better still, child, to give in now, to cut your losses, and I think under these new circumstances that perhaps you will.

My assurance of a good post still stands. You also know how welcome you would be in my household.

In the near future I will send you details of the will, also all personal effects of your uncle.

Meanwhile, Peta, I urge you to use common sense, even though your heart advises a different course. It is a hard fact in life that everything is based on hard facts, and the hard fact for you is that there will be absolutely no money available, except perhaps a small loan which you may be able to raise because of your prospects later on, but which I would not advise, for some years.

There was a chatty talk of the district in which she had grown up, messages from his wife, then Sincerely Yours.

Peta put the letter down and audibly groaned. She had nothing. Nothing at all. The fee she had received for Omar must have disappeared by now, and if not there would be precious little left. She had no idea of Australian rates for work, but she suspected they would not be less than English ones, and she knew that those stables could not have been built out of air.

Then there was the fodder to be kept up. Everything to be kept up. Then how could she stop on with Helen and not pay her way?

Again Peta groaned.

Fancy whickered, and in spite of herself Peta gave a small rueful smile. Always Fancy had seemed to sense her mood, to offer comfort. Going across to the horse, she pressed against his shoulder and found comfort now. In a few minutes she was on him as she had been earlier, only saddleless now, just Fancy and Peta, and the two of them were headed for the valley to blow away cobwebs once more.

This time money cobwebs, Peta laughed.

That laugh was to be Peta's last for many hours. She was to wonder afterwards if she had foreseen the nightmare before her whether she would still have ridden so blithely into trouble. Yet she knew she still would have done exactly what she did do, for to leave a pony in the straits that she found ... or rather Fancy found ... the little roan would have been repugnant to her.

At post-mortems it could ... and might ... be said, and she was aware of this as it all happened, that it would have been much more prudent to seek help. But help from where? Goa was the nearest place, and it was eight miles away, and the roan was in desperate circumstances.

Scarcely had the rider and horse left the stable than Fancy, gently but nonetheless determinedly, had taken off on his own account. Peta remembered occasions in Kinrow when Fancy also had taken over, and always there had been a reason for it. A sticky patch. A rabbit hole. *Something.* Now Fancy sniffed the air, pricked his ears, then deliberately picked a certain direction.

It was the same fern glade as earlier, but now the air seemed even greener, probably because the winter sun was much further to the west and shadows were deepening that green hue – I must watch for the signs of dusk, Peta told herself. But a few minutes afterwards she forgot her precautions as Fancy stopped, listened, whickered. Then, ears pricking and nose trembling, plunged headlong into the bush. As he was usually a careful horse, Peta did not restrain him even though the twigs and brambles cut mercilessly at her legs. Undoubtedly Fancy had received an answer to his whicker, she thought, an answer not heard by human ears, and he knew what he was about.

But it took ten minutes for Peta to know what Fancy had heard. Evidently the answer to his whickering was not forthcoming any more, for Fancy stood hesitant, then tried small glen after small glen, every tiny concealed dent of every join of the lower foothills, and then, whickering triumphantly this time, found what he sought.

Peta found it with him. The little half-dead roan. At first she thought of quicksands, then knew that had that been the case the pony would have disappeared long ago, for now she was remembering that faint noise earlier today down here, that tiny alarm that had worried Fancy to the extent of not wanting to return to the stud. And I, regretted Peta, saw to it that Fancy came up against his will. No, no quicksands, for as Peta could see in the fast-gathering shadows ... did Tasmanian nights always come quickly like this? ... there was no sign of squelch or mud.

But there was something else ... and cautiously Peta went forward, holding Fancy well back.

Peering down, she caught her breath in horror. Nat Trentham had told her of the quicksands he had not experienced, but he had also told her of the old mine shafts that he had.

Also the little roan had experienced them. Peta saw this and groaned. For the position could not possibly be worse. The road had fallen down but not through. It was still caught up in a flimsy but detaining scaffolding, caught by a grotesquely twisted leg. But the leg was not broken for all its unnatural position, she could see that, though the pony had fallen in such a way that he could not right himself, and just as well, for heaven alone knew how deep was the digging beneath him.

How long had he been there, the pretty little strawberry fellow? And though the leg was not broken, was it strained and bruised? Then what of the fetlock? The tendons? Had the roan eaten or watered? If it had been here all day . . . last night . . . was it suffering catarrhal fever? Was it even now moribund?

Fearing that Fancy's concern could land the three of them at the bottom of the digging, Peta tethered the horse some feet back, then cautiously she circled the hole. It was not a wide aperture, consequently very dark within since it trapped no light, so it was impossible to ascertain how far down the digging had gone. Searching around, Peta found a pebble and slid it in. It was with relief that she heard the splash fairly soon, so at any rate it was not abysmally deep, and yet, she warned herself, it could still be quite a hole down there and rain have filled it up.

She stood considering. She wanted to act and she knew from Fancy's whicker behind her that he was impatient for action, too, but she had to go carefully, for even though the little roan was caught there in discomfort and pain, better to be like that, and to remain exposed to the extreme chill that was now creeping over the glen, than to move irrationally and send the poor beast to the bottom where it could be wounded mortally . . . possibly drown.

Before absolute darkness set in she had to find out more about the pit. It could be deep. It could be shallow. The odds were on depth, but on the other hand diggers . . . often capricious . . . sometimes left off and started somewhere else. This seemed quite unlikely by the scaffolding, but one could still hope.

Her hope was rewarded. The digging was not shallow, but the part where the roan had managed to tangle itself was on the very edge of the pit and above fairly shallow ground. It helped, though very little, unless . . . and Peta shivered at the thought of what she had to do . . . the bottom of this particular digging was reached in stages more like a beach reaching out to sea, shallow, less shallow, deep. In other words not deep instantly as properly dug pits are.

Well, there was only one way to find out, and that was why she had shivered. She had to try out for herself.

The first step in made her think again of the quicksands she had discarded, for on closer contact she found that there *was* squelch and mud, but, the slime that encompassed her only went to her ankles and she had no trouble to break free. Another step, another probing, and her spirits rising a little. Yes, the digging had a bank around it, and if she could lower the roan it would only be to the shallow ooze where she now stood.

To make sure she inspected it all a second time. There was no margin for error, but she was confident that unless the pony panicked and threshed around there was little risk of it missing the shallow edge and plunging into the pit, and she did not think the poor beast would find the energy to move; at any rate it would be so cramped it would be temporarily lamed even without physical injury.

It was odd, she thought as she probed and prodded to make absolutely certain that such a digging had been made in the first place, but diggers change their minds and earth can look more promising further on just as grass can look greener in another field.

Yes, she was quite satisfied that the encircling ooze was distasteful but not dangerous. Probably, she told herself, because it *was* ooze and not dry, eroded, crumbling ground.

Now to release the roan. She dragged some bushes and placed them as a reminding barrier of where the pit actually began. They would bear no weight and she was sharply aware of it, but somehow they seemed to make a safety fence for her. Further than that, she rehearsed, we must not go. On a second thought she broke off more bushes, big stout ones this time with long branches that could be pulled along the ground. She pulled her own muscles doing it, cut her hands, smashed her nails, but eventually she found and placed the solid branches she needed for what she proposed to do, and then she was ready for the next move.

One thing, she should have no difficulty with the pony. He seemed barely alive, he did not move as she stood on tiptoes in the mud and felt quickly around him, discovered which rigging entrapped him and considered how it could be lowered.

It all went off better than she would have dared hope. The rigging gave way easily to her push and collapsed inwards in the same direction as she had placed the long branches. The roan slid rather than fell to the bank below. Now Fancy had to help ... though a rope, Peta thought ruefully, would have made it quicker than bending over almost to the ground from Fancy's back as she held grimly to the branches and Fancy pulled ... and pulled ...

The pain to her arms made her cry out, but she still did not let the branches go.

The pony was small, thank heaven, quite light, the mud had not had time to fasten around the burden, and after a few moments of the worst agony she could remember, Peta forgot her pain in triumph. The roan was out!

No need to have worried over a distraught animal. The little fellow lay where Fancy had hauled him, the leg un-tangled now, and, she believed, unbroken, but obviously pulled and painfully cut, and the pony, for some time, any-way, limp and lifeless.

Peta went back first to the pit, for disturbed ground, she knew, can sometimes open up, and if there was a chance of this she and Fancy had to haul the roan for another yard or so. But it seemed undisturbed and she felt confident in leaving the dragging at that.

She came back to the pony. It was certainly not dead but certainly extremely distressed, and as she looked at it, it started to shiver violently. That was understandable with shock and chill.

What to do now? Again she thought of Goa ... she could ride Fancy across ... but a second look at the roan, and probably the last tonight if the darkness kept up this rapidly, convinced her that if she was to save the animal, she had to do it herself. There was to be no time to seek help, only time to go up to Garo and grab what she would need, then come back again. Everything depended on the next hour. The pony had to have warmth, medication ... possibly food, for some of the exhaustion could be from hunger as well as exposure and injury, and she did not know how long the little fellow had been trapped.

She fluffed some of the softer branches around him for shelter, took off her jacket and placed it on as well, then addressed Fancy.

'You've got to come with me because I'll have a lot to carry. Also I'm depending on you to find the way back.'

Fancy whickered as though he understood. Uncle Claud had always said that horses had no great intelligence but wonderful memories and charitable natures. Well, memory and kindness were what were needed now.

It was biting cold by now, but that fact, though emphasized by the absence of her jacket, did not reach Peta in her urgency to get up to Garo and then back.

Another fuss around the little roan, more leaves . . . was there another garment she could take off and leave for extra warmth? . . . then a talk to Fancy once more, an appeal to him to know the way back again, a final pat to the patient, and the rider and horse were going up the valley.

As Fancy plodded the steep rise, Peta thought progressively. There was no telephone, so short of racing over the miles to Goa no hope of alerting Nat Trentham. She could, of course, ride out to the road linking with the Murchison Highway, but it was almost as far as Goa, and after she got there she would have to wait for a passing car, and in winter, the off season, it could be a long wait. No, she had to see this through herself.

All right then, what did she pick up at Garo and bring back? Much worse, what was there to pick up? Mentally she ticked things off. Every rug and rag that she could find and that Fancy could carry. Water . . . unfortunately cold, for there was no time to heat any. Then first-aid . . . that would have to be everything she could push in a bag in as long as it took her to grab it up. Uncle's favourite kaolin would be the thing, only it had to be softened in boiling water, so that was out. But she had other salves and ointments. A torch, of course. The lantern she had brought out from Kinrow. Tweezers. Boracic powder. Bandages.

Probably, too, the roan was suffering a chill. That required steaming . . . also out . . . but she had brought a supply of drops to see her through the sea journeys, and she would use them instead. Fever? That could happen. She had antibiotics by her also, and would bring them along.

For the rest, a little wearily, she simply didn't know. She had better grab some fodder for Fancy, and even for the roan if by some miracle he showed vast improvement and wanted to eat, and, seeing she would be no good if she weren't on top herself, whatever was left from her lunch. Also she must put on every sweater she could, pull on more socks.

Fancy came unerringly into the Garo paddock, stopped at the stable door. He was so understanding she knew she did not even have to tether him. As she ran inside and grabbed and stored, she heard him marking time for her return. She made more haste. If Fancy felt it was that urgent to get back she knew it must be so. She came out and bundled the load on him and scrambled up herself.

No cantering now, no taking of fences or logs, just a sober descent by her grey, once at the bottom a sniff to check where the injured roan had been left.

Peta switched on the torch, then lit the lantern. As far as she was able to in the still insufficient light she again checked the animal. The primary thing was exposure, she thought, but with the rugs she had brought and the friction she intended to try she felt she could attack that. Immediately, though, she must check for breaks once again. She checked, the pony making no protest, but not through absence of pain, she knew, but because the unfortunate little fellow was beyond even a whimper. There was definitely no sprain ... she felt sure of that ... but the leg that had been caught so grotesquely was pulled and needed circulation, after that a bandage to hold it normally.

She set to work expertly, for this was something she had often done at Kinrow. Before Kinrow to her own ponies at home. She massaged gently yet firmly, manipulating the limb back to its normal position. After ten minutes of this she applied the bandage from the outside edge up the distressed muscle beyond it, then down again. She remembered Uncle's preference of binding slack rather than too tight. When she was finished she cushioned the distressed limb on one of the folded rugs.

Now she got busy on the many cut surfaces the pony had

suffered. She felt the methylated spirits that Uncle Claud had used primarily on wounds might be too severe in this circumstance, and, since kaolin was out, adopted zinc oxide instead.

The roan was sniffing wretchedly, and she knew that a good steaming was called for, but next to that, it had to be drops. They were easy to administer ... indeed, the whole procedure was quite saddeningly easy, for a well pony would have protested, but the roan was beyond that. That made her indecision as to whether to try the antibiotic she had on her or not all the more difficult. Animals, she knew, could be as allergic as man, and because it was so easy to medicate the poor little thing, she hesitated, wondering whether it was safe or not.

Fortunately, for her indecision might have continued, the roan began shaking more feverishly than it had before, so Peta administered the medication without more ado, massaged each joint, covering it when she was finished, covered again wholly with the rest of the rugs, moistened the dry mouth, then said helplessly aloud, 'That's that.'

She switched off the torch ... she might need it urgently later ... then after a while the lantern as well, for she did not know how much fuel it stored. She stood a while wondering dare she light a fire ... she had brought matches ... whether, anyway, the wood would catch on in this wet glen ... if it did whether there was danger of the fire spreading.

In the end she decided against it. The roan needed warmth, but a fire would only warm one side of it, and she could not risk moving the animal a second time. Besides, her attention would have to be on it, and any attention left over, for she felt quite depleted, had to be on the patient, and getting the patient through the night. Also ... for with inactivity a realization of the biting cold had hit her ... getting herself through as well.

She called to Fancy and he came obediently. After a few minutes he lay down and she leaned against him. She wondered what time it was. Probably very early. That meant a long, long evening. She shivered. Now that both the torch and the lantern were extinguished she could not tell whether the complete blackness above her was because of the tent of trees obscuring everything else, or whether it was a moonless, starless night. All she was aware of was darkness, a *dark* darkness that she had never known before in her life.

There was an uncanny silence, too, no scuttling, scurrying, rustling as one would expect in the bush. She found herself listening so intently that her ears hurt. In the end she flashed on the torch and saw the tall trees bending over her, almost as though they would take her up. In the eerie light the fluted branches seemed thin ghostly fingers, the big dark mass of tree-trunks some unearthly shape.

She turned in a little panic to the roan. He was quite still under the pile of rugs, but breathing. She turned to Fancy and he looked solemnly back at her. A little ashamed of herself, she urged, 'Sleep, Fancy. I'm going to,' and switched off again.

A score of times through that unforgettable night she repeated that performance. Once she took out the remainder of her sandwiches and made a pretence of eating. Her eyes, accustomed at last to obscurity, found a silver lining to a cloud ... she supposed it was a cloud ... and she knew that the moon was coming up. However, it only made it worse for it established the earliness of the night. It also lit up in fitful glimmers the shapes of the bush around ... the thin reaching fingers of the trees. Yet somehow or other, and how she would never know, the night went.

The first she realized of its going was Fancy getting up and stamping his hooves, moving around. By the time she had un-cramped herself sufficiently to move, too, there was a thin smear of yellow buttering the top of the hill that dipped into the glen.

She got to her feet and moved around, too. When a little circulation had returned to her frozen limbs she went nervously to the roan. She had not asked any miracle except the miracle of its living through the night, but as she parted the rugs she saw that more than she had asked had happened. The pony was still manifestly ill, but the fever was not nearly so high, the breathing was easier, the limb in its normal position seemed fairly relaxed. There was no sign, though it was early yet, of course, of any inflammation of the roan's many wounds.

Encouraged, excited, she went through last night's procedure all over again. The check for breaks once more ... in daylight now, for the thin buttering of light had broadened and deepened ... the manipulation, massage, the rebandaging, the attention to the wounds. Again the drops. Although the roan showed no allergy, she did not repeat the antibiotic. She moistened the mouth again, then once more covered him up.

She did everything again three hours later, still not daring to leave for help. And then at noon, kneeling beside the roan to wet his mouth once more, to her joy he pushed his nose past her to pull at some grass.

'Fancy,' she called gladly, 'he wants to eat. Fancy!'

Fancy's whicker came at the same time as an incredulous: 'Damn my eyes ... it's not true!'

Nat Trentham stood there.

CHAPTER SIX

WHAT happened after that, Peta was not to experience, that is experience knowledgeably; she was only to be told.

Told first by Helen as the doctor took her temperature, told next by Nat Trentham as he sat on the edge of the bed and looked estimatingly at her.

Which bed? That was the first thing that Peta established ... and thankfully. She was in her own bed this time ... well, her bed, anyway, at Lavender House.

'I thought you might consider it too much of a good thing if I put you up at Goa a second time,' Nat had drawled after he had come in when Helen had gone out. 'Was I right?'

'Would it have been too much of a good thing for you?' Peta had come back daringly.

'The lady finds enough spirit for repartee. I think she is recovering.'

'You haven't answered the question.'

'You want an answer?'

'Of course.'

'Then it's No. No, it's not too much of a good thing. Satisfied?'

Angry with herself for having baited him and got an answer that left her at his mercy, left her disconcerted, Peta had diverted, 'Helen has told me what's happened. Around noon you came over to Garo from Goa for something, saw signs in the stable of a quick visit and a quicker departure, saw things missing, saw Fancy missing ... then decided there was something up. You reconnoitred and—' She shrugged. 'After looking up and seeing you standing in the glen,' she resumed, 'I can remember nothing at all.'

'You seem to have a penchant for doing that, for passing out. Why?'

'I've done it only twice. The first time I knocked myself out and the second—'

'*I* knocked you out?' he queried in mock seriousness. 'You looked up and registered "Nat" and promptly blacked out so that now I'm flattered, if embarrassed?'

'Don't be ridiculous!'

'I won't.' He nodded a promising head. 'I feel tempted, but I still won't. For down in that glen you put up an effort that won't be forgotten, my girl.'

'Now I'm embarrassed.'

'You should be kissed,' he said. He said it so simply and directly it could have been for belief, for *real,* but she knew it wasn't, of course.

Flushed, and aware of it, she muttered, 'Helen has told me how I keeled over.'

'Yes, I had three of you on my hands then.'

'Three?'

'Fancy was whickering his head off. Trying resuscitation with a rough tongue.'

'The dear boy!' she smiled.

'I shooed the dear boy off.'

'Actually,' Peta corrected, 'you put me in front of you on Fancy and came up to Garo.'

'Changing to the car and taking you pronto to Goa where I collected Hans.'

'And Hans brought me in to Helen while you looked after the roan?'

'You've got it right.' He felt for his makings, remembered he was in a sickroom and pulled his hand back. Peta hid a little smile. She knew now that the events of yesterday and last night had caught up with her and that the moment of Nat Trentham's appearance had happened at the same moment as her collapse.

'You were a limp ribbon,' Helen had described, 'right up to Garo, on to Goa, then to here.'

'I remember coming to for a few moments,' demurred Peta.

'And being promptly put out again,' said Helen. 'I considered complete relaxation the best move. I gave you a shot, Peta my dear.'

'Have I pneumonia or anything? It was terribly cold.'

'It was freezing cold, but you haven't pneumonia. You must be tough, for all your elf size.'

'Just as well for Fancy,' Peta said fondly, 'for my weight, although elf, plus Nat's must have been quite an ordeal.'

She had left her questions about the little roan for Trentham, who would know more.

'He belongs to a family of Dobetts around here. They breed bread and butter stuff. I think I spoke about that before. General horses which are still moderately in demand. They' – his lips tightened – 'could do with a few hard lessons, though I think one at least has been given.'

'You tackled them over the roan?'

'It had been missing for two days. Two days in this terrain at this time of year.' Nat had sworn angrily. 'They're careless. Not uncaring, perhaps, but careless. I don't think' – with satisfaction – 'they'll be quite so careless again.'

'What happened?'

'What your eyes saw. The little fellow got out, wandered

around, then managed to get himself trapped in the old shaft . . . there's dozens of them everywhere. That's why first of all you must see to your fences.'

'I will,' avowed Peta soberly. Then she remembered Mr. Gillett's letter and bit her lip.

'What is it?' asked Nat.

'Nothing.'

'Oh, come off it.' He had seen the bitten lip.

'Nothing.'

'All right,' he soothed, 'Helen told me you are still under some degree of sedation, so I won't probe till later.'

'Neither now nor later,' Peta found voice to say.

'We'll see.' After a tap on the door from Helen saying time was up he had risen from the bed – but stood looking down a long moment at Peta. Then unexpectedly, not even time for her to turn her head away, he bent over and kissed her lips.

'I said you should have that done to you.' He forestalled anything she might have said. Turning at once, he went out, and as he pulled the door she heard him rustling for his makings.

And what did he do outside the door as well as roll that cigarette? she wondered. – Kiss Helen? There would have been ample time to, for it was quite a while before Helen came in.

'Surgery,' she explained . . . which could have been true, and on the other hand untrue.

As though I care! Peta thought.

Helen sat where Nat had sat on the edge of the bed.

'Nat seems to think something is worrying you,' she said without preamble.

'So he asks you to find out?'

'No. But he did say you'd never tell him. *Is* there something, Peta?'

'Everything.' All at once Peta decided to tell her, tell anybody. After all, money, complete lack of, could not be kept secret for long. She reported briefly the terms of the will.

'A will can always be contested,' advised Helen.

117

'I wouldn't care to do that. I have every respect for Uncle Claud's wisdom.'

'Then at least arrangements can be made for advance monies to be drawn upon,' suggested Helen next.

'I suppose so. But it takes time, doesn't it, and – Well, Helen, here I am in your bed and being tended by you, and I can't even pay you. It's as simple – and desolating – as that.'

'I'm not desolated.'

'Then I am.'

'Which certainly worries me. I can prescribe all I can, but I can't prescribe against desolation. You must snap out of it, Peta.'

'I'm dependant.'

'Physically at the moment, yes.'

'And financially all my moments. Don't think, Helen, that a money miracle will happen, because it can't. Not the way the wheels of the law grind.'

'You are in a bad way!' smiled Helen. 'Will it help if I tell you that Nat rather guessed this situation and has a solution?'

'Stablehand at Goa or some such charity?'

'Nat never gives something for nothing, never deals in charity,' said Helen firmly.

'Well, *you* should know.'

If Helen got the import she did not betray it.

'Yes, I know,' she said quite unemotionally.

'Well,' asked Peta, breaking a small silence, 'is it employment?'

'Yes. And you'll have to work for him, don't worry.'

'Work for Nat Trentham?'

'Yes.'

'Then I do worry. I'd sooner work elsewhere.'

'Peta, there's nothing in this village, we're not a Hobart or Launceston. I should say that Nat would be the only one with a job to offer. It's either that, my dear, or—'

'Forfeit Garo?'

'I wasn't going to say anything so drastic, though you would have to, wouldn't you, unless you found some other means to hang on.'

'I could go to one of the cities for employment.'

'Who would look after your horses?'

'Mr. Trentham might.'

'He certainly would ... but at a price. What I'm trying to tell you, Peta, is that Nat will do anything, but not for nothing. Everyone always has to pull their weight. That was why ...' Another silence, rather hollow this time.

Peta broke it. 'If there's nothing wrong with me,' she said, closing the matter as far as she was concerned, 'I'll get up.'

'Tomorrow,' stipulated Helen.

'Doctor's orders – or Trentham's?' Under her breath Peta asked herself: 'Or are they both the same?'

'You take your pick, darling,' Helen answered, and she breezed out.

'I'll defy both of them,' Peta resolved. 'I'll just lie doggo for a while, then I'll get up.'

But the night before was not to be so easily dismissed; she slipped off to sleep in that waiting period, woke up later in a nightmare, believing the three of them, the roan, Fancy and herself, were slipping down the shaft in the glen, slipping down to slimy oblivion, and when Helen came in and literally ordered her to lie still, she obeyed, and at length went, without nightmares this time, off to sleep.

She was up for breakfast the following day, feeling as fit as ever, and was ladling out the porridge when the phone went. She took it up, expecting a call for Helen, but answered a call for herself. From Nat.

'How's the patient?'

'Thriving.'

'Ready for work again, eh?'

A pause from Peta, then: 'I haven't any work. I'm at a standstill. I haven't any money.' – Well, better to be frank; also, if she didn't tell, then Helen would.

'You hadn't all along,' he reminded her succinctly.

'I had – prospects. Now I haven't ... at least not till I'm twenty-five.'

'That letter, was it?' He spoke matter-of-factly. 'And

that was why you went racing blindly down the glen and eventually found the roan.'

'In a way ... though Fancy and I have always blown away cobwebs in a canter. Also, Fancy had picked up the roan's scent when we were down there before. How is the pony?'

'Recovering rapidly in his padded cell.'

'Padded?' she echoed.

'Well, the best wall-to-wall straw. A heater as well.'

'Do the Dobbetts go in for such luxuries?'

'No, but I do.'

'You have him there?'

'Yes. But I never do anything without my price. The roan ... with a suitable offer ... was my demand from the Dobbetts, the alternative to be a bad report higher up on the whole lamentable business.'

'I thought,' inserted Peta, a little put out, 'that it was I who performed the actions down there.'

'I haven't come to that. I was, of course, only representing you, seeing you weren't in a position to act for yourself.' A little pause, then: 'The roan is now yours.'

'So are Omar, Bess, Fancy – and the other three waiting to finish quarantine,' said Peta unhappily.

'You can always sell.' His voice was maddeningly cheery. 'In fact you'll have to, won't you, unless something crops up.'

'Like a job from the Lord of Goa?'

'So that's what I am.' He chuckled. He did not deny he had a job for her.

'Look,' advised Peta definitely, 'I want no charity. Oh, I know you don't deal in it ... Helen has explained that. I know a man, and a woman, is expected to turn in a good job. But you'd still never have thought of me, would you, unless this position had cropped up?'

'Which position? Be more explicit. The position of the money, lack of, or the position of your quite outstanding performance down there in the glen? If the latter is the case, you're quite right. I might never have wanted you on the payroll as urgently as I want you now had you not proved your quite remarkable worth. Look, I can't explain it over the phone. But it's something I've been thinking of doing, and Helen has been urging me, for some time. But it needs another hand with mine ... a good reliable hand. Yours. Prior to the roan affair I might have passed you over as not quite good enough ...'

'Pony girl.'

'But now I want you,' he ignored. 'In fact there's no one else I can think of who will fit the bill.'

'It sounds very mysterious.'

'It isn't ... but it's an innovation for me, and I like to start a new thing in a best possible way.' He waited a moment. 'Are you really well?'

'I said I was thriving.'

'Then jump into your clothes and be ready when I pull up in exactly half an hour.'

'Where are we going? To the place of assignment?'

'That's a long way from here. No, we're going to discuss it together away from Lavender House, and seeing you cheated me out of Redmarley, you owe me this day.'

'A day ... and much more.' She remembered again her straitened circumstances.

'I'll tender a bill,' he promised cheerfully. 'Might even make it a year. A lifetime. Meanwhile, be ready.'

'I'll have to ask Helen.'

Helen, who was passing the phone at that moment, said, 'That's Nat, isn't it? You're O.K.'

He must have heard, for he said, 'Right, girl. In half an hour. Don't dress up. We're going south.'

'South.' Peta sat down to eat her breakfast. She announced it to Helen and Hans.

'Queenstown. Mount Lyell,' nodded Helen. 'It's a near-perfect run, Peta. Enjoy yourself.'

'I don't think it's meant as enjoyment, it's to tell me about this post.'

'Take it,' advised Helen.

'I suppose I have to.'

'Then take it with grace, Peta,' advised Helen. She wore a little frown this morning. Her lips were tight. Her glance flicked across the table to Hans. 'Take everything with grace. I'm sure' – a deliberate pause – 'that that would be the case with Gretel.'

'Would it be?' Peta asked Hans, hoping to lighten the air which was becoming a little thick and she did not know why, nor evidently, from his usually pleased, placid expression, did Hans. 'Is your Gretel full of serenity and grace?'

'Ser-en-ity? Grace? My Gretel? Oh, yes, yes.' The answer was warm and loving.

Helen clattered her cup into her saucer with unneccessary vigour. 'I've stacks to do today.' She got up quite abruptly. 'Emulate Gretel, Peta.' She went out of the door.

'What is that?' asked Hans curiously. 'That em-u-late?'

'Helen means for me to be the same. The same as Elisabeta.'

'But that could not be so,' said Hans definitely. 'No one could be like Gretel, not for me.'

Helen was coming down the passage at that moment, and her steps stopped. Looking up, Peta saw that she was standing there quite pale. She herself sat stirring her coffee too long, puzzling, puzzling, puzzling over this entire ridiculous position ... Helen with an 'understanding' with Nat and openly admitting it, but still pale at a word from Hans. Oh, yes, Peta had no doubt that that 'No one could be like Gretel for me' had been the cause of the abrupt pause in her steps. It was all beyond her, and she stirred abstractedly, not realizing the brew had grown cold.

Nat's imperious toot of the horn brought her jumping to her feet. She knew that that man would frown on tardiness. She poured the untouched brew into the sink, rinsed the cup, then ran in to put on her coat and tie round a scarf.

At his third toot she ran out of the house. He had not got out of the car, but he had the door open for her. The moment she climbed in, he took off.

'You're in a great hurry,' Peta remarked a little resentfully.

'That little lack of courtesy was tit for tat for being late.'

'Barely.'

'*Late*. Dreaming again? Gazing into golden meadows?'

'Fields,' she said . . . but she did not admit that she *had* been pondering or he would have demanded the subject of her conjectures . . . have wormed it out of her in his inimitable way. And Peta could not hear herself saying: 'I was wondering why you and Helen are so platonic, for neither of you appear to possess natures like that.'

Fortunately he did not pursue the subject, he put his mind and energy to driving, for the road at this particular juncture demanded his full atttention, curving as it did between soaring mountains, then crossing gorges and bridging rivers.

'Here it's not another England,' he said, for there were none of the idyllic pastoral scenes that she experienced every day on the road into Helen's, those orchards, colonial cottages, ivy-hung churches. 'Here it's no-man's-land.'

'Yet beautiful.'

'I find it so.' He seemed pleased, though he did not say so, that she did, too.

They continued through rain-forest and fern gullies into Roseberry, a town, Nat said, of zinc. Here Peta saw the warning of quicksands; she also saw spectacular aerial ropeways of bucket conveyors feeding the ore to the refinery plant.

Zeehan came next, once 'The Silver City', ten thousand people to today's six hundred, and, Nat informed her, with six men to each woman. There had been a tramway once, a daily newspaper, and a Gaiety Theatre where Melba had appeared.

'They must have been wonderful days.' Peta was caught up with the nostalgic atmosphere of the old town.

'The six men to one woman?' Nat reached for his makings, then, finding them, instructed Peta in the rolling of cigarettes as he sped on to Queenstown. She made a lamentable job of it, and, pulling up, he tidied it for a while, then gave up and started afresh with a new smoke.

'You're no dab hand,' he told her. As he rolled expertly he told her what to expect in a few miles.

'I should let it burst on you, but anticipation is almost as pleasurable as realization. It's a splendour you can't forget, those sudden rock shapes in chocolate, pink and cream. Copper was mined first and it has yellowed the landscape, but when the afternoon sun is on the rocks there's purple, green and grey as well, in fact every spectrum shade you can think up in a dream.'

He started off again and neither of them spoke until suddenly out of the rain-forests rose eroded heights, looking, Peta thought at first, like the setting for an outer-space story, except that the colouring was beautiful beyond words, every Arabian Nights hue, as Nat Trentham had said. The outlines were lovely as well for a harsh place, for a mining city must be harsh, the modelling of the steep hills were as soft as a poem.

'It's up to you now.' Nat Trentham had drawn up the car so that Peta could feast her eyes on the coloured cliff-sides. 'Do you want to inspect the Smelters or do you want to watch the sun showing what it can do with outcrops of rock?'

'That, of course,' said Peta eagerly. 'Forget the Smelters.'

She sat back, looking first at the delicate shades and then at the bold. 'Such colour! Such contrast! I have never seen anything like it before. I've been told that at Alice Springs—'

'All the Inland,' nodded Nat. 'Through all the red heart of Australia, though that red heart should have burnt orange, crimson, indigo and purple added to it. But I'm glad you spoke about Alice, and the Inland, because that's what I want to talk about now.'

'Yes?' Peta said abstractedly, her attention still on the Arabian Nights scene being enacted for her.

'It's to do with that proposition I mentioned.'

Now she did listen. She turned surprised eyes to him. The Inland of Australia, but this was no Insider ... wasn't that what they were called? ... he was an Apple Islander (his own words) and a late Kentuckian.

'That's true.' – Would he never fail to know what she was thinking? – 'I know as much of Centralia as you do. But Helen has given me the taste. Oh, no, not for myself ... taste a Tasmanian apple, and, like Adam, you're tossed for

124

all time . . . but for a try-out with the "boys".'

'What are you talking about?' Peta asked.

'Helen is all for Goa becoming a racing stud, and I must admit that the thought does attract. However, I've never done it before, and I'd like to creep up on it, not burst in like a tyro.'

'In other words,' deduced Peta shrewdly, 'you want to come in winning.'

'How well you know me!' he came back. 'You must have studied me quite hard.'

'Well' . . . her cheeks were hot . . . 'aren't I right?'

'You couldn't be more right. In short when I enter the Melbourne Cup I intend to win it.' His tone was flippant, but she knew her words had been true; this man had to succeed, once he set his mind on something he did it. And won.

'Helen believes there's no proving ground like an outback race meeting. And that's where I intend to prove myself. With Big Kim.'

She knew Big Kim of Goa, a brown gelding, large as his name implied, but it was not the prospects of Big Kim as a racer that widened her eyes, it was the idea of this large Nathaniel Trentham thinking of riding him, substantial though the gelding was.

'No, no . . .' impatiently . . . 'I'll have him ridden, of course, but, according to Helen, even if I was the rider no brows would be raised. Not at the Downs.'

'You think Big Kim has prospects?'

'Good prospects.'

'How do you think he'll travel and adjust?'

'Excellently . . . with a stablemate.'

'Who?'

He was rolling his cigarette, licking the edges together. 'Fancy.'

'Fancy?' she exclaimed.

'At a fee, of course.' A slight bow to Peta.

'But Fancy isn't a racer.'

'*Stablemate*, I said. I've been through all my "boys" and there's no one who's suitable. Your Fancy has a particularly equable nature . . . I noted his behaviour with the little roan. All the horses like him, and I feel sure that Big Kim would suffer no homesickness with Fancy . . . at a fee, of course . . . by his side.'

'So that's the position you have to offer me. I'm to rent out Fancy.'

'That's part of the position. The other part demands more activity.' A pause. 'I want you to travel, too. As the hand.'

'I've had as much experience as you in actual racing,' she reminded him.

'Then we'll be a good pair.'

'You mean – you mean you would be going as well?'

'How else' . . . he was lighting the cigarette now . . . 'could I find out if I had racing material in me?' When she was silent he came in abruptly, 'Is my presence worrying you, I really mean my *future* presence? Then be of good heart, Miss Milford . . . or should it be of good social conscience? It's a "done" thing, Helen assures me, you'll find yourself by no means the only girl strapper. I'm not the first one to try himself out in a country meeting and not the first one to take a helper of the fairer sex.'

'Are you only doing it because of Fancy? Am I just something that comes along with Fancy?'

'Look,' he said impatiently, 'you need the job, I need you. Do you have to tear it to pieces like this?'

'I just don't want—'

'Charity,' he forestalled her. 'You've said so before. But I want you. Your performance with the roan convinced me that if I was to try myself out, as Helen urges, it had to be with someone reliable at my side. Someone who could at a pinch—'

'Yes?' she asked as he paused.

'Bring a sick horse back to life.' He said it bluntly, but the eyes he turned to her were warm. 'You're no "pony girl", young woman, you're—'

'Yes?'

'It'll keep.' – It sounded like that, but it didn't make sense. As he told her her salary, other details, Peta felt around that 'it'll keep' and wondered what it meant.

Then she heard: 'Tuesday week' from Nat.

'How do we go?'

'We fly right up.'

'Is there a direct plane from here?'

He grinned. 'If you charter one.'

'Wouldn't that be terribly expensive?'

'Not for the four of us, and not considered in the terms of experience gained. I mean, this is a first lesson for me, and no lessons of any course are free.'

'Will you take a jockey with you?'

'Helen says there'll be plenty available.' He smoked a few moments. 'Well, Miss Milford?'

'Thank you for asking me,' she said simply. 'I'd like to go.'

At once he put down the cigarette, then put his big hand on hers. 'Right, partner,' he smiled.

'Though we're not, are we?' she reminded him. 'You're employing me.'

'You're Fancy's owner.'

'But Fancy isn't racing.'

'Without Fancy there'd be no race. All right then, *under-ling*. Is that better?'

'Must you go from one extreme to the other?'

'No,' he said. Then he added: 'But I'd like to.' As she turned to him, confused, he switched on the ignition. 'If you've had enough of colour we'll go down to the pub for a bite.'

'I'd never have enough of this colour.'

'All the same we have a fair trek home, and I like to travel stoked.' He descended into Queenstown, Orr Street, the main thoroughfare, still retaining much of its wild-west air as when it was the queen of the rugged West Coast, most of the buildings unchanged from last century, the old wooden hotel into which he took her still with many of its ancient furnishings and fixtures. It was, thought Peta, like stepping into the past.

They kept away from the subject of horses during the meal. Nat told Peta how Queenstown only existed now for the Mount Lyell Mine.

'Ore, gold, silver, iron pyrites,' he said. 'Once it was a Lady Luck city; last century a mine was sold for a hundred pounds and a week after it changed hands for twelve hundred. But now everything is stable. Better, no doubt, if less romantic.'

They came out again to the Wild West street, Nat drove Peta up to a vantage point to gaze once more on the unforgettable colours, then they retraced their tracks . . . crossing Pea Soup Creek to come into Zeehan, plunging into the rain-forests and fern gullies to spin into Roseberry, and then home.

'I'll keep you posted as to the Downs Meeting,' Nat said as they approached Lavender House. 'Have you liked today?'

'I've loved it. Thank you.'

'Thank you for accepting my offer. Also, thank you from the roan. I promised the little chap I'd say that.'

'I must come and see him.'

'I would take you today, only I think you must have had enough.' He slackened the pace of the car. 'Looks like Helen has enough, too.' He took a hand off the wheel to wave it in the direction of the porch of Lavender House.

Helen was standing there on the top of the landing with an old man standing several steps beneath her.

'Patient?' asked Nat idly.

'Doesn't look like one. Helen would have him in the surgery.'

'Well, if that's the case she'll be pleased to have you here with her. Some of these swaggies—'

'Swaggies?' Peta queried.

' "Once a jolly swagman camped by a billabong",' he reminded her. 'Travellers . . . bagmen . . . roveabouts . . . choose your own name.'

'He looks too old for that.'

'All of them are old. The youngies have no veneration for Matilda.'

'I really meant too old for camping out in this Tasmanian climate,' said Peta.

'And you're right at that. We never did get many. It's a

128

different thing to carry your swag Up Top. The nights flower there, not come with skies clipped out like a cameo.'

Peta said, 'With silver scissors.'

'So you've noticed our nights.' He seemed pleased as he had before. 'I don't think I need stay to protect you two girls,' he went on. 'He seems quite harmless, poor old boy. Thank you again, Miss Milford. I'll be seeing you.' He leaned across and opened the door and waited for her to get out. When she did so, he closed the door, saluted her, called out 'All serene?' to Helen, and, receiving confirmation, spun smoothly out of the drive.

Peta turned to a rather bemused Helen, who met her eyes across the top of the old man's silvery hair, and mouthed distinctly: 'What to do?'

Helen drew Peta into the hall, the old man still standing on the bottom step.

'Name of Josef, or so it sounds ... can't decipher the surname ... and he wants to stay and work in the garden.'

'Helen, you already have a gardener twice a week.'

'I know, but Jim could have him raking leaves or something of the sort.'

'Your garden isn't that big; it's also an easy one to maintain. Jim mightn't care about another on the staff.'

'He can set him oiling the wheelbarrow, sharpening the tools. Jim will like it; he'll be head man.'

'It's not for me to say.' Peta wondered why Helen had drawn her aside like this if she already had made up her mind.

Helen was silent a moment, then she said, 'I thought we could fix that annexe to the garage quarters where Hans has his flat.'

Now Peta saw the trend. Helen was not just contemplating finding employment for the old man, she was considering accommodating him as well, and she wanted Peta's encouragement.

'I don't know what to say,' Peta answered the unasked question. 'I mean you don't know him.'

Another pause from Helen, then:

'You'll think I'm mad, but I feel that I don't *not* know

him.' Helen hunched her shoulders. 'Anyway, what harm could the old fellow do?'

'I didn't mean it like that. Of course he'd do no harm. But on the other hand why should you put yourself out?'

'Peta, it's crazy, but I'll be more put out not accepting him.' Helen looked steadily ... and a little pleadingly ... at Peta.

'Then, darling, do it,' Peta said impulsively. 'I'll help you. Let's do it at once.'

'You mean it?'

'Of course.'

'Then that's all I want. I'll bring him in and give him a cup of tea and we'll fix the annexe up between us.' Helen went out to the old man, brought him in and settled him at the table with the teapot that was always standing ready to be filled, and a large cup. In the annexe, as they put up the spare bed together, tucked in sheets, piled on blankets, Helen explained.

'We get few swaggies ... in fact all Australia gets few now ... the only ones you really see are six-inch dolls in the souvenir shops done up with tucker bag, fly-veil and rolled blanket. Another pillow, Peta.'

'Is this man a bagman?' – Nat had said that, swagman, traveller, roveabout.

Helen gave a brief laugh. 'You tell me what he is and I'll tell you. I can only follow a word here and there.'

'A migrant?'

'It's doubtful at his age. Still, he's *here*, isn't he?'

'What nationality?'

'Another rug, Peta. He's old and it's a cold corner.'

'What nationality?' Peta asked again, not prepared for the sudden vivid flood of colour in Helen's cheeks.

'The same as – Hans. I've discovered that much, anyway. Coincidence, isn't it?' She did not wait for a reply but unfolded a mat and put it beside the bed. 'There, he should be snug.'

'Very snug, and, I think, very fortunate.' A pause. 'Helen, why are you doing it?'

'Putting a roof over a poor old man's tired silvery head?'

130

'Oh, I know *you* would do that, because you're Helen, but you could do it with a cheque, not the personal touch, yet you're making it the personal touch.'

The doctor adjusted the pillow. 'No answer,' she admitted at length. 'I just want to, somehow.' Again she looked pleadingly at Peta, and Peta patted her arm.

'That's all right,' she smiled. 'Let's settle Josef in his new digs.'

On the way back to the house the telephone rang, and Helen veered first to the surgery to answer it. Peta went on into the house, but at the door of the kitchen she paused.

The old man was not sitting where they had put him, he was circling the room, looking closely at everything. As Peta watched he took down a photograph that Helen had hung of one of her friends and peered at it closely.

For a while Peta stood watching. Whatever else he was, Josef was not quite the character that Helen had made of him. And yet, although his movements were secretive, somehow you could not couple anything that was wrong with them. Wrong with him. Aware that she should report the odd behaviour to Helen, yet somehow unable to, Peta stepped back, gave an indicative cough, allowed the old man sufficient time to sit down at the table again, then came into the room. She smiled at him and he smiled nervously back. She spoke a few words, but he could not follow her. That, anyway, was true enough, she thought, watching the dark eyes that did not show any understanding. Well, it was Helen's concern, not hers. Perhaps, though, she should tell Nat when she went to Goa.

Helen came in, and took the old man down to his room. When she returned she wore a little frown.

'Sorry you patted the cat?' asked Peta wryly.

'No . . . he's all right, but – well, he seems to be looking for something. It's mad, I know, but he looks round all the time. Did you get any impression of the sort?'

'Yes,' said Peta, wondering what Helen would say if she told her why she had got the same impression, that her own impression had been fact, that the old man had been searching the room.

Helen brewed up and they sat down at the table together. The doctor seemed preoccupied and Peta tried to break into her abstraction with a cheerful: 'Don't regret your charity, Helen, he's quite harmless, and anyway, you have a man about the house.'

'That,' inserted Helen a little grimly, 'I have not.'

'What about Hansel?'

'He's gone to Hobart to do some specialized reading. He'll be away' – a little abrupt laugh – 'for all the period *you'll* be away, Peta.'

'How did anyone know I'd be away?'

'Nat told us.'

'How would he know when I didn't know myself?'

'That's Nat. I've no doubt he had officially arranged for you for that Inland trip even before he mentioned it.'

'Very confident, isn't he?' Peta's voice was acid.

'Very. And it always comes off.' The laugh this time was fond.

'What did you mean,' asked Peta next, mentally contrasting the affectionate laugh to the previous rather bitter one, 'by saying that Hans will be away for all the period that I'll be away?'

'It's the same reason that I first had you here, my pet. Convention. Propriety. Social obligation. Or' – there was no laugh now but a certain stoniness – 'a conforming to what – Gretel thinks.'

'Elisabeta?'

'That's correct. Elisabeta, who is Gretel.'

They both drank for a while, then, drawing a long breath, Peta dared: 'Is Hans – anything to you, Helen?'

Helen turned direct brown eyes to Peta's and answered, 'Why do you ask? Does it show?'

'Frankly, it does . . . in bits.'

'Then for heaven's sake tell me if it does more than that, for he has this girl already, hasn't he?'

'I asked you something, Helen,' Peta said gently.

'Then – then yes, he is something. I don't know how it all happened, unless—'

'Yes?'

132

'Rebound ... that's the horrid word, isn't it? I was just getting over something ... someone ... else. They say it often happens like that.'

'But it wasn't *really* that, was it?' Peta was still gentle – yet persistent. 'Even had this someone been here as well it would have been Hans.'

'Peta, don't talk like that. You know as well as I do that Hans has that other girl, that she's coming over here.'

'But *if*,' persisted Peta.

'I don't know. I just don't know. I'd have to see him ... this man I was going to marry, I mean ... again. See them both together. You see, I came across from the mainland to marry him, only – well, he wasn't here. He had gone on. I suppose pride should have pushed out love, except there's a simple factor: there isn't any pride in love. When Nat insisted that I remain here—'

'Oh, yes, and that's another thing. Where does Nat Trentham come in?'

'He doesn't.'

'You have an "understanding". He has said so. You've said so yourself.'

'A very big understanding. You see, he's the brother of the man I came to marry but who left before we could keep that pact.'

'Then you could have married the brother who stayed,' ventured Peta.

'I could have – if he'd asked me. Also if it had ever been that way to him, or to me. No, you have it all quite wrong, Peta. Nat Trentham is my best friend.'

'I see.' Peta was quiet a long moment ... but not near so quiet her sudden sharp awareness of her heart thumping madly. She had a feeling of heaviness taken away from her, a feather lightness where there had been crippling weight. So ridiculous, she endeavoured to check the racing heart, this means nothing to me. All along I noticed that platonic attitude between Helen and Nat. Everything is just the same as it was. Nothing is altered. – But still her heart raced.

On an impulse she leaned over and touched Helen's hand. 'When I say to you that I understand, I *do*, Helen.

You see, in a way . . . in a sort of way . . . I'm in the same boat myself.' Yet only in the way, she thought, that someone was not waiting for me either, but it was quite different with Peter, he had no money to wait, he had to leave because I was so long. Also, I have no two thoughts about him . . . not like Helen with her man. I loved Peter, I love Peter, I will always love Peter. Past, present, future. It's just that every day it's seeming further away. More like a dream. But opposed to that dream, unlike Helen again, there is no present reality for me. And there never will be.

Nothing real. All at once she felt the treacherous pink flooding her cheeks, and she turned her head away, hoping Helen had not noticed. The reality, her heart was beating. *The reality*. The reality that is—

'Thank you, Peta,' Helen was saying. She had not noticed the flushed cheeks. The moment passed without comment. 'When Hans comes,' went on Helen, 'as no doubt he always will come if there is a third present' – a little shrug – 'he'll be able to speak with old Josef. Meanwhile let's try to bring a smile to that poor old boy. He's rather a sad sack, isn't he?'

'Yes,' said Peta a little evasively, for as well as being sad, Josef had a purpose, though what it could be apart from theft, and she simply couldn't couple theft with that old man, she could not say.

'Tell me about what lies before me, Helen,' she diverted, leaving the subject of Josef.

'The Inside?'

'Yes.'

The doctor gave her a sly look and said:

'Somewhere in Australia where the ants and lizards play,
And a thousand fresh mosquitoes replace each one you
   slay,
O, take me off to 'Frisco . . . let me hear the mission bell,
For this misbegotten country is a substitute for Hell.'

She poured another cup for both of them. 'That was written by an American.'

'Nat?'

'Nat is Australian.'

'But late American.'

'The blue grass country, not 'Frisco,' said Helen. 'No, it was not Nat. The Inside will be as new to him as it will be to you. And I'm not telling you, Peta, I'm letting you discover for yourself.'

'Ants, lizards and mosquitoes.'

'Dust and flies as well,' grinned Helen. 'I'm running out now to see old Granny Davis. Keep an eye on our senior citizen, Peta, on Josef.' She went along to the surgery and a few moments afterwards Peta heard her back out the car.

She washed the tea things, then went out into the garden. It would soon be dark and she wondered if she should set a place for Josef to eat in the kitchen with them tonight or whether Helen would take his meals down. Seeing he was to work in the garden she rather expected he might be there, and looked around, but there was no old man. A little alarmed, for after all what did they know of him ... or of his health ... Peta went down to the annexe. She gave a little tap on the door, but there was no response. She pushed it quietly ... perhaps he was resting on his bed. But Josef was not there.

Perhaps he had not realized that Helen intended keeping him and had pushed on – but no, his few personal things were still there. She went outside again.

Next to the annexe was Hansel's 'flat' and had she not seen Josef's head through the window she would have gone past, not dreaming the old man would trespass into the room. But now she stopped, very annoyed. Josef had no right to intrude like this!

She turned the door handle without preamble and went into the room after him.

'Josef,' she said quite sternly, prepared to chide him, even though he mightn't know one word that she said. But the face he turned to her was so pathetic, so appealing, and – yes, so innocent, she found she had not the heart.

He said something she couldn't comprehend and moved obediently to the door. But before he went he gave a long look at the photograph on Hansel's shelf. It was a photograph of a middle-aged woman with a sweet expression and rather tired eyes. – 'My mama,' Hans had once said with a tender smile.

He's lonely, decided Peta with pity of old Josef. That's why he was looking at Helen's photograph in the kitchen. He wants people near him, he wants contact, either visual or actual.

Softening to him, even though she was aware that loneliness should never be an excuse for trespass, Peta leaned across, and, taking his arm, led him outside again. He said something that again she could not follow and went to his room.

When Helen came back from her call she said she would take an evening tray down to Josef ... but she came back again with it untouched.

'Asleep,' she said tolerantly, and Peta decided not to speak about the old fellow.

But she spoke about him several days later to Nat Trentham, for though her attention was now taken up in getting ready for the northern trip, being briefed in what would be expected of her up there, what to take for both herself and the horses, she still could not fail to notice Josef's behaviour. The odd thing about it, she puzzled, was that Helen never noticed. It was as though, for the doctor, he had fitted almost as an older relative in the house.

But Peta noticed. She saw his glance as it wandered here and there. She felt ... sensed ... his waiting for something.

For what could old Josef be waiting?

She was sitting on the Goa fence watching Nat put Kim through his paces the day she decided to speak on the subject. It was a crisp late-winter afternoon, rather what she imagined of the American blue grass country where Nat also had done what he was doing now. Reluctantly she had to admit to herself that Goa needed more land, particularly if Nat went on with his plans to race as well as breed. The field in which Nat was cantering Kim was not nearly big enough. The fences needed removing, the whole spread out. But for that, Garo would have to go.

Big Kim was good, but to Peta's mind not all that remarkable. She felt sure that Omar could have beaten him with ease. She said this as Trentham and Big Kim came up to the fence.

'Of course,' agreed Nat Trentham. 'I've never said otherwise, have I?'

'Then—'

'Then why didn't I choose Omar?' He took out his makings. 'Could be your fee stopping me, I'm not made of money, and it's not as if' – a quick teasing glance – 'ours is a family affair, what's yours is mine, all that stuff. Oh, no' . . . as she did not speak . . . 'cash on the dot as befits strangers for our Miss Milford.'

'That's unfair!' She had flushed dully, but it was not the acquisitive trait he had accused her of, it was that teasing 'family affair'.

'I agree,' he said at once, 'you're certainly not money-hungry, otherwise you would have sold me Garo weeks ago. Unless' – he was spreading the tobacco now – 'you're holding off for a high price.'

'Mr. Trentham—' she began.

'It'll have to be Nat, I'm afraid, Peta.' For the first time he spoke to her by her name. 'Anyone who calls anyone with a Mister in front of it Up Top is, according to Helen, well and truly barred.'

'Nat,' she amended . . . and was annoyed that she gulped over it . . . 'you could have had Omar.'

'I know.' His answer was instant and warm. 'But I wanted to try out for Goa, not Garo, and Big Kim was the best on hand. No, you've done your bit and more letting me take along Fancy.'

'I'm being paid for it.'

'Isn't there a price on everything?' He was lighting a match now and over his fingers tented to guard the flame she met his eyes and there was a flicker in them as well.

A little uneasily she changed the subject to Josef.

'You knew that Hans had gone to Hobart for special reading?'

'Yes.'

'Will Helen be all right while I'm away?'

137

'She's always been all right before.'

'But she has this old man there.'

'So I hear. What is it, Peta? Don't you like him?'

'I like him very much, but—'

'Yes?' Now the faintly bantering eyes were keen and probing.

She told him how she had seen Josef peering round the house . . . seen him in Hansel's room.

'He's old and he's strange to the place,' he excused.

'Yes,' she agreed, but still not satisfied.

'Look, I'll have a word with the fellow.'

'I wish you would, Nat,' she appreciated.

Anything Nathaniel Trentham said he would do, she knew, he did. And promptly. That night, as she might have guessed, he telephoned her.

'All clear?' he asked first.

'Yes.'

'Josef not there?'

'He stops in the annexe. Anyway, he wouldn't follow any conversation.'

'No, I don't think he would, but I managed, if to no great guns, to follow *him*.'

'Yes, Nat?'

'Helen out of earshot? She's not the nervous kind, but it could make her jumpy if she knew we were checking for her.'

'She's out on a call.'

'Then here it is: Josef is an old traveller . . . or something of the sort. That took a while to establish, but eventually I found it out. He's been all over Australia . . . I don't know why . . . and Tasmania is his last fling. He'll be going on eventually, he has no intention of burdening anyone, he has a little cash, but he would like to stay on to speak to our Hansel before he goes.'

'But why?'

'Same country, I suppose. Wouldn't you be like that on foreign soil?'

'But how does he know about Hans?'

'Look, I knew about every Australian within a hundred

138

miles when I was a Kentuckian.'

'I expect so,' agreed Peta. 'Well, so long as you think there's nothing to worry about.'

'Nothing at all,' breezed Nat. 'My only worries now are that you have everything in control for the next few weeks.'

'We checked that yesterday.'

'I meant for yourself, not the "boys". Has Helen briefed you?'

'Every detail. She has told me that though the Downs is hundreds of miles from everywhere I'm not to take things cheaply, that the women think nothing of even getting a Paris gown for the event, though I, of course, will have no need to worry about that, I'll be in jodhpurs and shirt.'

'Not at night you won't.' His rejoinder was sharp. 'There'll be balls, lady, and I don't want you trousered for the moonlight waltz.'

'What difference could it make to you?'

'The difference would be to Miss Milford. I simply wouldn't cross the room, bow and ask you for the honour.'

'Then most assuredly I must send to Paris, mustn't I?'

'It doesn't matter about Paris just so long as it's a skirt.'

'Mini?' she taunted.

'You know what,' his voice came back lazily over the wire, 'I doubt if you were ever spanked.'

'Well,' said Peta crisply after a few moments of counting to ten to control herself, 'is that all?'

'We, and the float, take off at piccaninny daylight on Tuesday for Launceston ... travel out to the drome and pick up our ferry craft. Estimated time of arrival at the Downs I don't know as yet, but' – she heard him lighting a match and she could see the hand tenting the flame but not tenting that flicker in the eyes above the flame – 'time will tell.' A pause. 'Will that do?'

'Yes. Thank you, Mr.— Thank you – Nat.'

'. . . Is it so damn hard?' His voice came a little roughly now. 'You don't seem to be getting any better at it.'

She could think of no reply, for it *wasn't* getting easier, for some reason every time she said 'Nat', her throat contracted.

'Peta, are you there?'

'Yes.'

'I asked you was it so hard?'

She was aware that she was clutching the receiver so tightly that her fingers ached. Lightly she borrowed his own words to bridge a situation that was awkward and she did not know why it should be awkward.

She tossed: 'Time will tell.'

CHAPTER SEVEN

ON this occasion Peta took care that she was ready to dash out the moment that Nat pulled up at Lavender House.

He was towing the float with Big Kim and Fancy and she was pleased to see it was a comfortable float, well protected from the weather but with good vision for the horses. Uncle Claud had always believed in unrestricted viewing for all concerned.

At the risk of Nat's impatience she went first to the float to speak with the 'boys' and to nuzzle Fancy, but when she came round to the utility he had the door open and he was grinning.

'I see I'm put in my place.' He shut the door after her.

'Well—' she began.

'It's all right, Peta, I'd do the same.' He let out the clutch and went carefully forward, only gaining speed on the Murchison Highway, and then keeping it steady and smooth so that the horses would have a good trip.

Obviously they enjoyed it. Every time that Peta peered back she had to report eager heads into wind, not missing a trick.

'I only hope they keep that up,' said Nat.

'Well, they can't in the plane.'

'I meant their general wellbeing, and I was thinking more of the Inland. It will be a much different climate from Goa. However, at this time of year it should not be too hot, and, according to Helen, the nights drop right down.'

They passed through blackwood and sassafras forests, mills milling myrtle and shedding dark sawdust, pine plantations for pineboard, farms with mail bags hanging out for the mailman, windmills, orchards and pea-fields. In a few months, Nat told her, the bush would be a riot of Christmas Joy, Fair Slippers and Waratah.

Nat took the utility straight up to Burnie, delightful in its green slopes setting with the sea on the other side. Ulverstone and Devonport were reached and passed ... 'I did think of Devon for a charter, there's quite an airfield there, but I know this Western Junction firm,' said Nat, nodding for Peta to try her hand again at rolling a cigarette for him. He told her as she folded and moulded and he turned and twisted of places out of Devonport called the Promised Land and Nowhere Else. 'I wonder,' he ruminated, 'if there's Nowhere Else nowhere else.'

He commended, 'You're doing all right' of the rolling, and wasted no time this time in correcting the cigarette finally to throw it away, instead he placed it between his lips and lit it, then he turned into a road she remembered ... in reverse ... when she had first arrived in Tasmania, fields under different crops making a chequered pattern, tanglewood fences and hawthorn hedges.

Everything went smoothly at the airport. The charter ... a Bristol Freighter ... was waiting, the crew of two pilots and wireless operator-navigator ready, the horses were led in and secured, then Peta and Nat were seated. The engines whirred, the plane taxied, they rose above the chequered fields and pine plantations and within minutes had left the coast. Beneath them the Bass Strait lay like a looking glass in bright blue, but it must have been height that gave the illusion of complete calm, for Peta could see whitecaps here and there.

The coast spread out again ... the mainland now. 'Australia,' presented Nat by Peta's side, 'not Britain Down Under any more.'

Cities appeared and disappeared, flats, mountains, rivers ... and then the harsh yellows of the arid regions began, the great salt pans, the clay pans, and soon after the pans the incredulous colours of the great deserts, the Arabian Night reds, purples and blues.

They put down briefly at Alice Springs, but only time to attend the horses and snatch a cup of tea. Peta would have loved to have seen that unique town, centre of the earth's oldest country, but she had to be content with just looking at it nestling in its oasis of ranges from the outside, for there were hundreds of miles yet to do.

'The country's too big,' smiled one of the pilots, 'we should give it back again.'

Now Peta could not take her eyes from the scene below, spinifex, saltbush, red ochre sand, vivid purple patches of Calamity Jane, delicate snow patches of wild white iris, rocks rising out of sand and taking on unbelievable hues. But most of all she was caught up with space ... limitless space. It was like a wide-screen film everywhere you turned.

Nat went along and checked Big Kim and Fancy and came back smiling.

'I believe they're enjoying it as much as we are. Anyway, our pilot tells me we'll be landing within the half hour.'

The engines changed rhythm before that. Peering down, Peta complained she could see nothing that promised journey's end.

'You wouldn't,' advised Nat. 'Compared to our holdings it's rather large ... a thousand square miles at least ... though up here that's only average-size. Elsey is three million acres – there you are, civilization at last!'

At first all Peta could trace were scattered buildings, iron roofs. Then she saw the homestead spreading out as only a home with countless space for spreading would spread. Red roof. Verandahs all round. An encircling oasis of trees ... some of them, the second pilot called to them, citrus. – 'There's assured supplies of bore water here,' he said.

They were down now, and the homesteaders were coming eagerly out to meet them in station jeeps, behind them piccaninnies so fleet of foot that they arrived, by taking short cuts over the spinifex where the jeeps had to curve round it, almost at the same time.

'Is this the Downs?' Peta asked of Nat.

'Yes. But naturally on a thousand-mile square you need more than one hub. This particular hub is Narganoo, meaning red, but I reckon they've made a green paradise of it instead.'

'Where is the racecourse?'

'There isn't any.'

'But—'

'That part of the Downs is some seventy miles away yet.'

'Seventy?' she exclaimed.

He smiled. 'A mere bagatelle. It was Helen's suggestion that we put up ... at least *you* put up ... with the Fiedlers. The Downs centre will be crowded out by this. Incidentally, don't expect an established racecourse even there.'

Peta asked two questions at the same time. 'So these Fiedlers know I'm coming? Where will you be?'

'Does that look as though they don't know?' Nat waved his arm to the approaching jeeps. 'I've no doubt Mrs. Fiedler simply can't wait to see another woman. I hope you're well up on the latest in Bond Street. I'm going on to the Downs ... Downs proper ... to see how things are there. I'll take the boys ... by that I mean our crew as well as Kim and Fancy ... with me, and settle the horses at once. Later on in the week I'll settle you as well.' As Peta looked a little unhappy at being set down among strangers, he laughed, 'In five minutes you'll have known them all your life. Or so Helen assured me.'

Nat could not have been more right.

Mrs. Fiedler ... 'I'm Jenny, Peta ... yes, Helen wrote us your name' ... simply threw her arms around her, explaining breathlessly, 'Take no notice of this emotion, I've been pining for woman company. Roslyn is only eighty miles away, and that's next door up here, but it's eighty miles too far.' Then on top of the sentimental greeting she demanded, 'Are the skirts still as short as the ones David Jones sent me up? What did you bring for the ball? What's in and what's out? What colour lipstick is that? Would that perfume be—'

Nat burst out laughing and sought out Mr. Fiedler and

man talk.

The homestead was delightful, Peta thought, when the jeep pulled up at the front steps. A cool, green polished cement lounge-room with bamboo chairs, the rest of the floors of the house bare but with rag mats in bright colours. Her own room, when Jenny opened the door, was in orange chintz ... 'Somehow we have to keep to those colours up here,' said Jenny, 'it's a lion-coloured country, really. These particular tawny shades are not exactly what I wanted, but you have to order by mail and hope for the best.'

'I think you got the best,' praised Peta.

Tea was in an immense kitchen, the huge range at one end, the big table laden with scones and sponge cakes at the other ... 'Oh, no,' said Jenny as Peta looked with awed eyes at the display, 'we have a cook, and just now an excellent one.'

Nat waited for a cup, refusing Bert Fiedler's invitation to stop at Narganoo and drive over later in the week. 'After all,' Nat said, 'I've come to learn first and enjoy after.'

'I rather gathered that would be the idea,' nodded Bert Fiedler, 'so I have the truck and the float ready for you to take off. The track's not at all bad and you should make it in the light.'

Peta asked why couldn't the Bristol have gone right to the Downs and was rewarded with knowing smiles.

'There's not enough landing space?' she interpreted of the smiles.

'There's ample at ordinary times, but just now it's like Mascot ... London Airport for you, Peta ... planes popping in every few minutes.'

'From surrounding stations?'

Bert nodded. 'Also every state. This is the biggest picnic race of all. It's not the first time someone with his eye on a Melbourne Cup one day has limbered up first up here.' He grinned at Nat. 'I'm sorry you're not stopping,' he added. 'The male company I do have isn't as much up my alley as you would have been. City fellow doing the Downs for a feature article. He's out today with the Flying Doctor. Oh, well, I suppose a man can't be greedy. Not with a thousand-mile radius and eighty miles for a chat with your neighbour. You learn to appreciate all company then.'

Nat left after the tea, the pilots and wireless operator, having secured and protected the plane to their satisfaction, accompanying him.

'When do you want Peta delivered in?' called Bert Fiedler to Nat, as having checked the float with Big Kim and Fancy ensconced in it like princes, Nat got behind the wheel of the borrowed truck.

'In two days. By that time I should have found a suitable dig for her.'

'Two days!' Jenny's woebegone voice broke in.

'After all,' reasoned Nat, 'she's here to earn her keep. Well, b'seeing you.'

'B'seeing you,' they chorused, and Nat began the twisting track into the red ochre sand. They stood and watched him until the red showed no moving spot any more.

Jenny followed Peta to her room to exclaim over everything she had brought and now unpacked.

'Make no error about the Downs Races,' she said, 'not a woman there won't have been planning her rig for twelve months. Oh, it's lovely to have you here!'

Little by little Peta pieced together this whole fabulous race 'thing'. For miles around, she learned, there would not be an inch of the Downs ... Downs proper ... unoccupied. Station planes, station trucks and jeeps, caravans, tents. The commercial merry-go-rounds and hoop-las already would be there, the chocolate wheels, the shies, all hoping to snare before-meeting trade. Also pedlars. Hamburger men.

Then the official tea-tents run by the women would be up already. – 'I'm on the second day of the meeting,' Jenny said. 'I must show you my apron. Quite inadequate and absolutely foolish, of course ... imagine serving pots of tea and big corned beef doorstop sandwiches in pink lace ... but it's the occasion, not the purpose.'

Bert Fiedler wandered in and told Peta about the actual course.

'There's no rail, naturally, when you turn at the half

mile it's round a huddle of onlookers.'

'Isn't that dangerous?'

'Oh, yes.' Bert shrugged. 'Someone always gets hurt. But there's sure to be a doctor, and then there's the district nurse.'

'There's a ball every night,' put in Jenny. 'I've a dress for each. Come and see.'

'Women!' snorted Bert. 'Thank heaven I've this fellow here, even though I'd sooner your man.'

'My man?' Peta sought for words to explain, then decided not to, for Jenny was anxious to show Peta her own purchases, and Bert was listening now and nodding to himself.

'That's the doc's Cessna putting down. I'll send out the jeep.'

'Come on, Peta,' urged Jenny, 'it'll be twenty minutes before they're in.'

The two girls had just finished Jenny's third dress, whether it needed pearls or whether it should be left as it was, as the jeep panted up.

Bert's booming voice calling, 'Hi there, you two!' reverberated into Jenny's pretty room that although she had ordered by post and hoped for the best was still a triumph for Jenny Fiedler.

'Stopping for a meal, Doc?' Peta heard Bert. 'Good man! Come in, both of you, and make mud of that dust.' – Next the sound of glasses and bottles and man talk.

Peta went back to her own room and brushed up for the evening meal. Because she knew it would delight Jenny she changed into a pretty frock and took care with her hair. When the bell went she went down the passage to the green cement lounge where Bert was again plying drinks ... smaller ones, more elegant, chinking of ice, no doubt as a gesture to his wife.

'This is our Flying Doc, Chris Walters,' Bert introduced to Peta.

'This feller-me-lad is a city slicker, name of—'

'Peta! Of all people, Peta! *My* Peta!'

Out of the violet shadows of the corner of the big room

where he had been standing looking out of a window stepped a remembered figure.

'Peter!' Peta whispered back.

Aunt Alice once had told Peta that though most Australians were casual the Westerners were the most unsurprised of all. Peta was glad now that the Fiedlers were no exception, otherwise they could not have helped but stand and stare at Peta and Peter standing and staring at each other.

As it was Bert Fiedler only boomed cheerily, 'Met each other before? Good show!' The Flying Doctor held up his glass to both of them. Jenny, enjoying the rare social event so much that nothing else penetrated, simply smiled.

Ludy, one of Jenny's girls, came in with a tray of appetizers. Several had obviously disappeared between the kitchen and the lounge, for the spaces between showed, but no one minded, least of all Ludy who was trying to eat without giving herself away. The talk was general, and Peta was glad of that. There was a lot she had to say to Peter, but just now she could not have found a word.

Peter must have felt the same, for he only generalized, too. But his blue eyes meeting Peta's tawny ones over the cool green room said volumes.

Preoccupied, Peta came back to where she was at the sound of her name.

'Would you like that, Peta?' Bert Fiedler was asking.

'I . . . I'm afraid I was daydreaming.'

'On such a night as this.' Bert waved his arm to the window where a pansy dark sky was lighting up with stars so tropically close you felt you could pluck them if you stood on your toes. 'I can see,' said Bert, 'we'll have to find a young man for you, young woman. Daydreaming, indeed, on a night made for romance!'

Though she did not look at him Peta was aware that Peter was looking at her. Nights of romance . . . she remembered the nights on the ship.

'What were you asking me, Bert?' she inquired.

'It was really Doc asking, I just repeated it when you kept daydreaming.'

'And it was?'

The Flying Doctor said, 'A flip tomorrow. I have to go up to Cuppy Creek.'

'There'd be ample time,' put in Bert, 'you won't be wanted at the Downs for a few days yet.'

'I think it's an excellent idea,' Peter came in smoothly. 'Peta should see all she can. Thank you, Chris, we'll enjoy the Cook's Tour.'

The doctor was not over-pleased, and said a little bluntly, 'You weren't very enthusiastic today. I thought you'd had enough.'

'By no means. If I was quiet it was the material I was storing away. Cuppy Creek – I think I can get an article out of that. Rice, isn't it?'

Still short, the Flying Doctor said, 'Yes,' and took a long drink.

Jenny and Bert, if casual, were not insensitive. At once Bert made another round of the ice-chinking concoctions his wife had insisted upon to mark the occasion, saying plaintively as he did so that he'd sooner a beer. Jenny made an excuse and ran out to see how dinner was progressing, and came back soon afterwards to announce that it was ready, and for everyone to come.

'To please Mrs. Bert,' boomed Bert, and he came and put his arm out to Peta.

Jenny giggled as she accepted Peter's extended arm, and the doctor shrugged and took up a cushion and brought that.

'We're being ridiculous,' said Jenny, but she was enjoying herself, and she stood happily at the table while everyone applauded.

Everyone outside the window as well. The entire aboriginal staff had come up from the gully to look at Missus's candles, and their flashing teeth showed their delight. Jenny made no attempt to draw a curtain, and Peta loved her for this. The boys and girls lingered a while, then, either bored, or drawn by their own dinners cooking succulently over a eucalyptus fire, voted rib bones more enticing than the concoction Boss and Missus were having, and drifted off.

Jenny put out the electric light, her husband remarking appreciatively that they'd have to do this more often, it would be easy on the plant, and with only the creamy flicker of the candles the talk softened, left mundanities behind. The Flying Doctor became genial again with Peter, and Peter—

Across the table Peter looked at Peta. How often had she thought of this meeting, Peta asked herself, for she had always known that she and Peter would come together again.

Sometimes her dreams had *not* been 'candlelight' ones, they had been considered in searching daylight, as it were, considered in terms of *Why?* – Why did Peter fail to meet me? *Where?* – Where did Peter go? *When?* – When does he intend us to meet again?

But now in the candlelight, all the criticism, all the disappointment vanished. Vanished in that deep blue look of Peter's, that little tender smile flicking the corners of his mouth.

She felt the talk drift around and knew she did her share. But she knew, too, she was not really here, she was on the ship again, standing at the rails in Peter's arms. When would she be in those arms again?

After dinner there was coffee and liqueurs, even though Bert said sadly he would like a cup of tea, then they all sat in the green lounge, Bert asking the doctor about the Hapsleys whom he had visited today, was it true old Hap intended going in for cotton, remembering now and then to include Peter, and Jenny was plying Peta with eager 'outside' questions that Insiders long to know, and Peta was answering, even elaborating, and wondering how she did so, she felt so suddenly unreal.

Then Jenny was remembering that Hilly's piccaninny Marybell had a funny sort of rash, and would the doctor look at it before he turned in. Evidently, Peta gathered, the F.D. often stopped where he landed of a night. Well, there certainly would be ample room, these houses did not stint on space.

Bert went, too, with a lantern, for the plant stopped at

149

the house.

'We won't be long,' said Jenny. 'There's nightcaps yet. Oh, yes, I know you'd sooner beer, Bert, but it's going to be—' As she left the house her voice drifted away.

Across the wide green room Peter looked at Peta. Then he rose and moved towards her.

She had no awareness of rising as well, moving towards him. She only realized she must have done so when she felt the tender closure of his arms.

CHAPTER EIGHT

ALL the things she had to say were never said. The questions. The reproaches. The pleas for him to tell her his reasons so she could understand. The feeling that she had experienced of late that what had happened between them was becoming more unreal and dreamlike every day no longer was a dream. It was here. It was real. Real in Peter's arms.

'Poor Peter. Poor, darling Peter!' she heard herself whisper. 'You couldn't wait because you had no money.'

His lips in her hair, Peter whispered back, 'Yes.'

So nothing else was said. Or, Peta thought a little deliriously, needed to be said. Tomorrow he would tell her things ... she would tell him of Uncle Claud's death, how she was placed, but now nothing mattered except the nearness of Peter, a nearness made all the more delirious by the mystic, almost elusive beauty of the northern night, for they had moved instinctively to the verandah by now, the stars more brilliant than on the coast, the sky a deep blue cloth, a pheasant intoning 'Puss, puss' as he moved in the shadows, a wood pigeon crying a quaint 'Move-over-dear' ... 'Move over-dear'.

'Oh, this Inland!' Peta said, entranced.

'Oh, my Peta!' said Peter.

They moved apart as the Fiedlers and the Flying Doctor came back to the house.

'Thank heaven,' Jenny intoned. 'I've had a suspicion all along, but I wouldn't admit to it. I just couldn't have faced Hilly's pic having measles or pox, not at this time of the year. I mean they look forward to it even more than we do. Besides, Chris is such a disciplinarian he probably would have ruled the Races out for all of us.'

'I certainly would,' said Chris firmly. 'You would have started a major epidemic in there. But it's only an infant thing Marybell has, probably worsened by Jenny here herself. You would have done better to have left it alone, Sister Nightingale, than dab that harmless rash with antiseptic. It's a wonder you haven't started a dermatitis.'

'She'll kill us all before she's finished,' groaned Bert. 'Do you know what she's nightcapping us with? A fancy posset she read in the Women's Glossy. Bits of cucumber floating in it. All I want is—'

'A beer.' Jenny was beaming. 'I'm so relieved for Hilly we'll all have beer.'

'And throw the posset out?'

'That's not the name.'

'This drink by any other name would taste as less. Beer coming up.' Bert removed the thimble-sized glasses and brought out steins.

The night ended in laughter. Only when Peta lay in bed did the laughter give way to something else. An excitement. A joy. And yet withal ... and try though she did to dispel it, it still persisted ... somewhere in the excitement and joy a crying out, an awareness that it was all somehow second-best. Second-best?

The morning dawned blue and golden, but then most mornings in the Inside would dawn that way, Peta supposed.

'Though when it rains,' Jenny, who had come with a breakfast tray and remained to perch on Peta's bed, related, 'it certainly rains. The rivers run bankers. All sorts of beasties ... toads and things ... invade the house. But it's lovely to see the green creep over the desert. You actually *see* it, Peta. And the Jane and the iris paint the red ochre purple and white.'

'You love it, don't you, Jenny?'

'It's my place. And you?'

'I liked it at once.'

'Could it be your place?'

'I suppose so . . . with the man I loved.'

'I expect that would be true of any place. But failing the man?'

'Britain Down Under,' smiled Peta after some thought. 'That's what Nat called it.' — Nat. It seemed odd to find room for Nat in her thoughts that seemed bursting only with Peter.

'Apple Isle,' smiled Jenny. 'Lush. Green. The very opposite of Up Top. Oh, well, it takes all sorts. You'd better hop up after you've eaten. Our good doctor is a very painstaking man. Like time and tide he won't wait for anyone, even a beautiful girl.'

'Then he'll be safe,' laughed Peta.

'In that gown you showed me for the ball you'll be more than beautiful,' said Jenny. 'I'll go down and tell Chris you're on your way and to get out to the Cessna.'

When Peta came out to the verandah, Peter was already waiting for her. Bert directed one of the boys to drive them out to the home-made strip where Chris by this time was heating up the engine. As soon as they arrived he waved them aboard, and almost at once he took off, Peter not so keen as he had been last night, for the doctor had Peta beside him, and Peter in the rear seat.

'I work from Matabah Base,' recounted Chris, 'which being small makes me more or less a freelance, and able to stop over as I did last night. Now Boolalil Base is quite different. The F.D.s come home to roost every evening. Then, of course, if there's anything really big, we get Air Ambulance. There's a whole team on that. Pilot, two nurses, doc.' He looked down and said, 'You've seen all that before.' Peta looked and nodded at the salt and clay pans. 'But,' promised Chris, 'I'm going to show you something new.'

They passed over surfaces turned flame where the sun reached, and violet where it didn't. They went over a creek with actually crocodiles . . . yes, crocs, grinned Chris . . . sunning on the banks.

Then the doctor was turning southward again, or rather sou'west, to the rice he had promised Peta. From the air the alien crop made a breathtaking picture. Because they were in latitudes where all seasons were one season so growth perpetual there were varying stages to look down upon, from the first froth of green to the waist-high grass-like plants. It made a pretty mosaic, and Peta turned to Peter. He looked patently bored and said that articles on planting rice with your bare feet had been done so many times he would sit this one out.

'Only,' came in Chris crisply, 'here the seed is broadcast from the air in low altitude sweeps.' He circled Cuppy Creek, then put down beside a paddy field. 'Chief trouble here,' he related, 'is the Honker, or Pied Goose; he has a liking for rice. However, an extensive sanctuary with feed in plenty and no men with guns is overcoming that.'

Peta and Chris had got out of the Cessna to look at the crop, but Peter remained in the plane.

'Where does the water come from, Chris?' Peta was looking at the rice in its wet bed.

'Around these parts there are tropical monsoons between November and March. All the lower lying ground is inundated for months. I wish you could see the header in action, Peta, it can take off eight tons of grain in an hour. And that rice is needed, believe me. After all, it's the basic food of half the human race.'

'*You* should be writing that article,' said Peta with interest.

'Is there an article being written?' asked Chris drily.

'But of course. Peter is attached to – Peter is with—' Peta did not finish. Instead she pretended interest in the green lines of the bulrushes planted on the contoured banks of the rice bays. Peter, she thought, had not said what paper had commissioned this job.

They went back to the Cessna ... Peter asleep now ... and Chris criss-crossed to a peanut and sorghum project at a place called Wallenbibby. The homesteaders came out to meet them, the children staring shyly at Peta but falling all over the doctor whom they knew, as all the Inlanders knew, as a good friend. The father was anxious to know if Bert Fiedler had anything in the Cup. 'I've a spare quid in the kitty,' he grinned. But his wife was only interested in what Jenny and Peta were wearing.

Peta asked if she was going, too, and was answered with a surprised, 'Of course!'

Winging back to Narganoo Peta reminded herself that she must look up her own frock for the festivities ... she had not as yet taken it out of her bag. Seeing she was to be here several days she might as well let it hang, not huddle.

But when the jeep came out from Narganoo to bring Peta and Peter back to the homestead ... Chris was moving on to his base again ... Jenny was in it beside Bert and she was wearing a long face.

'You're to go in to the Downs. I'm not to have you as long as I anticipated. Oh, well, what's my bad luck is Roslyn's good luck. You'll be staying with the Blaineys. Mark oversees the same as Bert. Anyway, Peta, I'll see you at the ball.'

'Then that'll go for me, too, Peta,' said Peter. 'I'm going to keep inflicting myself on the good Fiedlers. Is that all right, Bert?'

Bert said of course, if that's what he wanted.

Feeling somehow embarrassed, Peta asked, 'How do I go in?'

'I've a truck leaving quite soon with some gear I promised the committee. You can go with Bill.'

While she was putting her things in her bag, Peter came in.

'Sorry I can't come with you,' he said ruefully. 'We haven't even had our talk yet, but the fact is I haven't any Downs digs.'

'Didn't your paper see to that?' said Peta indignantly.

'You know me, darling, never tied up. I'm freelancing, of course.'

Never tied up ... The three words stuck with Peta. Something in her expression must have reached Peter. He slipped his arm around her and said: 'The drummer, remember? We can't all be the same. I'm the one, darling, who steps to a different song.'

'Yes, Peter,' She waited till his arm slackened a little, then moved away.

'I'll see you at the ball, pet,' Peter said. 'We'll have the moonlight waltz.'

Someone else had said that, only he had put it differently. 'I don't want you trousered for the moonlight waltz,' had been the words.

Two keeping pace to different drums?

Bert called out soon afterwards that the truck was ready if Peta was, and she went out to a tearful Jenny in spite of the fact that they would all meet up again in several days.

'Not as a house visitor,' bemoaned Jenny. As Peter pretended to look hurt she added, 'Female of the species. It's been months, and now I only just get you, then have to give you away again.'

'My dear Jennifer, you've Ludy, Kitty, Hilly, Queenie—' began Bert.

'But no Peta. Oh, well, it's Roslyn's turn. See you at the ball, Peta.'

'Anyone would think,' inserted Bert, 'that that's all this function is – a ball. We'll see you, Peta, in the days that precede and follow as well.'

'But not in our ball dresses.' Jenny had the last say.

The truck revved up. Peta was hoisted in, then to waves not only from the two Fiedlers and Peter but the entire homestead from the oldest old man to the youngest piccaninny, they set off.

Peta wondered how the driver could decipher the track, there seemed tracks everywhere. But they were only windwaves, Bill told her, no wheel-ruts. Oh, yes, there were wheel-ruts here, they might look like sand but they were there and as easy to read as a marked highway. They lumbered through dark green clumps of spinifex interspersed with thickets of mulga and stands of desert oak, through miles of ochre red dust, past sandy river beds with nothing in them, past 'wurlies' ... old aboriginal watering places ... with pad-marks of dingoes, rabbits and kangaroos. Once they saw brumby camels, their colour against the sand making them almost indistinct, and once some overlanders with a mob, for not all the stock, said Bill, went on the road train or by air-lift even now.

Then at half dusk they came into the Downs, really only Narganoo again, Peta judged, but at this momentous week of the year a veritable little city, fairly humming already with stalls and sideshows, a rather reedy merry-go-round and an Afghan who strung his 'Latest Paris Creations' between two convenient gum saplings.

But it was the cars, jeeps, land-rovers, trucks, utilities, caravans, table-tops, the aircraft ranging from station Moths to charter planes that took Peta's breath away. Literally they covered miles of the Downs, people living in them, by them, under them. And more were arriving.

There was actually a minute hotel and a store here at the Downs proper, the hotel with swinging doors and a counter polished by elbows, the store a trading post with literally everything, and just now doing a fine trade.

Bill drove Peta straight to the Blaineys, where she was met with the same enthusiasm as at the Fiedlers, Roslyn as eager for company as Jenny, for though there were several more houses, she confided, they were company ones, and the company wives only visited now and then, preferring to live on the coast, so apart from Mrs. Villers of the store and the district nurse when she wasn't on call, that was all.

'Except,' relished Roslyn, 'for one week of the year.'

Roslyn had gone to the same trouble as Jenny, though it was a joy, not a trouble, for both of them. Peta knew this a second time as she sat at a charmingly set table.

Nat was on the other side of the table now; he had arrived soon after the truck had.

'Good trip in?' he had drawled.

'Wonderful.'

'Yes, I thought that. Like to change our own background for this?'

' I love this Inland, but down there is home.' He looked so smugly pleased that Peta added, 'Seeing it so resembles my real home, I meant.'

He shrugged at that and asked what she had done at

156

Narganoo. There seemed no need to tell him about Peter, so she didn't. She related the air-flip and the rice fields.

'It's a fabulous area,' said Nat. 'Once we had all the minerals down beneath and could smile tolerantly at their stock wealth and crop potential up here. But as well as that now every time they dig they find something. The lucky territory.' He took out his makings. 'Tomorrow,' he told her without preamble 'you can do some work.'

A little nettled, she answered, 'I had no intention of evading it.'

'Thought you might have gathered that idea with all the social activity around. However, that moonlight waltz is still on.'

'Wearing my jodhpurs?' She could not resist that.

'You won't,' he said confidently. 'You'll be like every other woman, dressed to kill.'

'Kill what?'

'Not what, who,' he corrected.

'Whom,' she corrected again. She added stiffly, 'I have no desire to slay.'

He gave a throaty little laugh, and, at Roslyn's bidding for dinner, overdid his bow as he presented his arm.

It was dinner by candlelight again, Roslyn as keen to capture a moment away from the trivial round as Jenny had been. Indeed, it could have been a repeat of Narganoo . . . except for the man across the table from Peta. No deep blue look now but bramble-coloured eyes probing, holding . . . challenging hers. Peta turned her own glance away.

The liqueurs and coffee came. They all went to sit on the verandah to look at the lights of the show people, of the visitors who had set up their canvas roof trees and lit them with hurricane lamps.

'It's so exciting!' thrilled Roslyn. 'Why can't it last all the year?'

Her husband grunted that after it was over and you faced the mess once was too much in a year.

'Old grump,' said Roslyn, and Nat added to that, 'Which *I* will be, too, tomorrow, if I don't hit the hay. I'll expect fitness from you as well, Miss Milford.' He rose, thanked his hosts, told Peta he expected her on the job bright and early.

'In jodhpurs or skirts?' Peta pertly inserted.

'In order' ... Nat ignored Peta's interruption ... 'that a good day's work can be done.'

'But tomorrow night is the ball,' rebuked Roslyn. 'She must stay home and prepare to be beautiful.'

'She is beautiful,' contributed Blainey gallantly.

All Nat said was a short, 'I'll be round at eight sharp.'

'These men!' despaired Roslyn. 'But he's terribly nice, isn't he?'

Peta said with secret feeling, 'Terribly.'

The show lights were off; the hurricane lamps were lowered and the Blaineys, too, went to bed.

Nat was around on the dot, but Peta saw to it that she was ready on the dot. In her jodhpurs and shirt she waited on the verandah, and was in his borrowed jeep before he could cut the engine.

His eyebrows rose up in mock surprise and he looked banteringly at her, but he made no comment, simply drove along the track to the improvised stables. He had secured a very favourable box right at the end of the row ... trust Mr. Nathaniel Trentham to do himself proud, thought Peta. But when she saw the fitness of the 'boys' she felt pleased that their manager had either 'wangled' or brought the best for them. The pair were thriving.

'What are my orders?' She was aware that he was awaiting her approbation and was determined not to praise him.

A little thinly he said, 'It's always orders from me, isn't it?'

'What else?'

'Well—' reaching for the makings – 'what appeals?'

A little desperately she evaded, 'A canter on Fancy.'

'I was referring to myself.'

'I'd still like a canter on Fancy.'

Quite thinly now he said, 'You'll have one after you practise out on Big Kim.'

'Big Kim? But—'

'He is racing, yes. And I've secured a jockey, yes. But I haven't anyone to give him trials, or exercise him. It was hard enough finding a rider, and I'm too heavy myself.'

'I'm not up to racers,' declined Peta.

'Then you better be,' he said bluntly. Immediately, though, he added encouragingly, 'You can do it. Don't forget I've watched you. I wouldn't dream of asking you if you couldn't.' As he was speaking he was bringing Big Kim out of the box, saddling him expertly. Not giving Peta any time to back out, he turned round and legged her up. Big Kim was a large horse and it seemed a long way to the ground. She started off carefully, then saw that though Big Kim was large, he was steady as a rock ... she might have known that Trentham would have taken no risks with his racer.

'Nor' ... now the man was actually running beside her ... 'with you.' He was laughing at her, at the thoughts he had read in her.

Peta gave Big Kim a signal and they started to race.

Nat stopped her the first time round. 'Ease up,' he ordered.

'You asked for a trial.'

'I got it ... Now just exercise Big Kim.'

'But—'

'Look here, the ground's not prepared, you could have a spill. As well as being disastrous for Kim it could be costly to me, especially with you claiming big compensation as well as my being landed with a bunged-up racer. Also, I don't want any totes seeing just how good Kim is.'

Peta could not resist agreeing excitedly, 'He *is* good, isn't he? I take back what I said about Omar being better.'

The man beneath her smiled up at her, and for a moment they were confederates, not enemies. 'Good, Peta,' he confirmed. 'So just take him easy for a few circuits, then come back and rub him down, and after that—'

'Fancy?'

'Fancy,' he agreed.

Peta cantered off.

The morning sped. Always conscientious, now Peta was

lit up with what could happen if Big Kim kept up his good performance. She rubbed him assiduously, spending so much time on him that only Fancy's little whicker of complaint put her stowing the dandy brushes away and turning to her own boy.

'Right you are, darling, your turn.'

She leapt up, her knees gripping Fancy's sides in the way they both liked to ride, then, her tawny hair fanning out in the wind that Fancy's speed coaxed out of the still air, they circled the improvised track.

When she did the second circuit, a man came out to help her dismount.

'Why, Peter!' she said in surprise.

He seemed excited about something, but everyone was excited just now.

'Peta, isn't this that Fancy you took me down to see on the ship?'

'And you were bored.' Peta rather wondered at herself answering that.

'I wanted to look at you instead,' he reminded her reproachfully.

'And now?' She *was* in a difficult mood, she thought a little self-censoriously.

'Now and always. But' – a little pause – 'your Fancy has speed. Peta, how would it be—'

There was a call for Peta to get Fancy out of the way of a string of horses, and she obeyed it at once. After she had rubbed down and tethered Fancy, watered and fed both the boys, she came out, not surprised that by this time Peter had gone.

Nat came along soon afterwards and insisted she go back to the Blaineys.

'No.' He held up his hand as she went to protest. 'I'm not a slavedriver. Besides—'

'Yes?'

'As well as skirts tonight I want a beautiful young woman in them,' he grinned, 'not an exhausted strapper!'

'I'll do my best.' Peta went a few steps, then added, 'Boss.'

'If you were a boy,' advised Nat, 'you would have been booted for impertinence.'

'But I'm not.'

'No.' A pause. 'You're not.'

She walked back to the Blaineys, enjoying the whirled bits of paper and the stirred-up dust that is part of every outdoor activity. But she knew, too, that the disturbed red ochre sand was covering her as well as everything else ... particularly her dark honey hair that seemed to take to ochre over-readily. She knew it would mean an hour longer in the Blainey bathroom to emerge her own colour again.

But Roslyn had anticipated this, and laid out shampoos and creams.

'We're both going to be really remarkable,' she bubbled. 'We'll show those Sydney slickers!'

And when the girls did come out at Mark's third exasperated call that they'd better be moving across to the hall if they wanted a seat, the hours proved worthwhile. Roslyn, brown-eyed, black-haired, was regal in rich burgundy lace, and Peta had chosen her favourite tawny gold again, interpreted this time in filmy chiffon. So awed that he did not remember to point out that he had been waiting for forty minutes, Mark took an arm of each girl.

The hall was an astonishment to Peta; she had expected nothing like this. Streamers, yes, paper lanterns, crepe made into flowers, balloons ... But never the trailing vines that the homesteads had sacrificed from their own porches, the barrels planted with large branches of native ti, ferns from jealously nurtured bush-houses standing in water in circles of wet lucky stones. Even a contrived waterfall that splashed musically and was illumined in greeny-blue light.

'It's wonderful!' Peta praised.

Roslyn, who had a lot to do with it, looked pleased and triumphant.

The orchestra struck up.

'Flown here,' said Roslyn in Peta's ear. 'This is our gala night. We spare no expense.'

'And this is my dance,' claimed Mark of his wife. 'I could add of that gown that you personally have spared no expense. But I won't. It's paid dividends. And I'm very proud.'

They whirled off, Peta smiling after them. She waved to Jenny in rose-pink silk and in the arms of an equally proud man.

The music ceased and the musicians waited for their first round of applause. As the clapping died, the notes crept in again, sweet more than provocative this time, subtle, haunting.

In the semi-light as all the lamps were lowered from two corners two men approached Peta. Not until they stood before her at the same time did they notice each other.

'Nat!' exclaimed Peter.

Nat said nothing, just looked at the other man. They both turned to Peta, and instinctively she rose.

Nat had spoken of this waltz. Peter had spoken. But Nat had spoken first. She had come to the Downs with Nat. Nat was the boss on this expedition. He directed and she complied. Everything pointed to her politely declining Peter and turning obediently to Nat. And perhaps she would have done so – but for the fierce anger that met her eyes when she raised her own to Nat's. Eyes like pinpoints in their bitter resentment. Eyes that promised a reckoning, not a dreamy waltz.

Turning deliberately, Peta slipped into Peter's waiting arms.

She heard Nat's sharp ejaculation at the same time as Peter's little laugh of triumph.

Then the other dancers were whirling around them, obscuring Peta even further than in the concealment of Peter's tight clasp.

'I'll never forget this moment.' Peter's lips were over Peta's ear. 'And not because of you, my beautiful, lovely though that thought is, but because it's my first real triumph over him, over the great Nathaniel.' He gave a low laugh. 'Thank you, Peta, for choosing me.'

'I didn't. I mean—'

'But you did, my sweet. You deliberately cut the great Nat and came to me. That's something I never dared hope for, but it happened just now.'

162

'I should have accepted Mr. Trentham,' said Peta uneasily.

'But you accepted Peter because you love Peter. You do, don't you, darling? You've just proved that.'

'I did love you,' said Peta uncertainly, 'but when the weeks and months went past——'

'I can explain that. In fact you've explained it yourself. Money, lack of. The opposite, incidentally, to Trentham, who has money, plenty of. But this is one time it was of no avail.' A tightening in Peter's already tight grasp.

'Peter, it was very rude of me. He spoke about this ball before you did.'

'You can't tell a heart what to do,' said Peter. 'That's why you're in my arms.'

'I'm here because I was frightened of him,' she corrected wretchedly. 'He – he's such an unpredictable man and I didn't want words.'

'You're wise as well as irresistible, my Peta, though I still don't believe you. You chose me because you love me. You wanted nothing of Nat.'

She felt as though she was dancing on leaden feet. Peter had never spent much time on words of love; even on moonlit nights on the ship those words had been, though precious, quite brief. She should have revelled in them now, revelled in Peter, but she felt heavy and lacklustre.

'I'll tell you the whole story if you must have it,' sighed Peter of her lack of enthusiasm, 'though there are lots of other things I'd sooner say.'

Somehow she didn't want to hear them, and yet she had lain awake at nights longing for such words. On the other hand she didn't want his story, either. Not now. She shook her head numbly, and Peter pressed her closer and said, 'I understand, my love, just relax.'

There would be other dances after this . . . a lot of them . . . country dances went on all night. She thought of one dance that would turn out a reckoning, for the eyes Nat Trentham had turned on her had spelled that out quite clearly. R-e-c-k-o-n-i-n-g. She gave a little shiver.

'Peta, sweetness?' queried Peter.

'I don't want to dance with him.'

'You're not going to. You're not leaving my side all the night. Tomorrow. Ever. Besides, I have something to ask of you.'

'No, not now, Peter.'

'It's not *that*.' Another closure of his arms. 'I know the answer to that already. It's ... Well, we'll leave it till later. Just dance now.' He whirled her round.

Peta need not have worried about a tall ... taller than Peter ... figure crossing the room to her, bowing sardonically. For Nat Trentham never came. She never saw him any more that night. She was not to see him, either, the next morning ... a message was to come with her breakfast. Miss Milford would not be needed at the stable. She could attend the races as a visitor and not an employee.

'In other words,' Roslyn had deciphered gleefully as she relayed the message, 'you dress up like I'm going to.'

In other words, Peta had deciphered for herself, keep away.

But all of that happened the next day, a day made more uneasy still by what Peter had asked of her later in the night, and what she in an unguarded moment had finally agreed upon.

'The purse is five hundred dollars,' Peter had said as he had put forward his pleas, 'and, darling, I could do with that.'

'But your articles ...' began Peta.

'Look, I was a fool to come up here – oh, I'm glad to heaven I did because of you, but monetarily, Peta, there's nothing here for me. I've not had one inspiration ... red ochre dust and wide open spaces aren't my cup of tea. I'll doubt if I'll produce one word.'

'But, Peter, it's wonderful here.'

'Not my variety of wonder. It's crude. It's – well, it's just not me.'

'Then why didn't you leave?'

A pause, a rueful pause, and then: 'Frankly, I'm broke. Dead broke. Even the few days with the Fiedlers was a handout in the position I am.'

'Oh, Peter!' she sighed.

'Yes, miserable, isn't it? But much more miserable for me to have to admit it. Yet' – a hunch of his shoulders – 'there you are.'

Peta said quietly, 'I can't help you. I haven't got round to tell you yet, but Uncle Claud died, and everything fell through.'

'Poor you as well as poor me,' proffered Peter. Then he said, 'You must at least get round to recounting how you hitched up with Nat.'

'He's my employer. Well, on this project, anyway.'

Peter smiled. 'What he is to me will surprise you. But it is, as I said, rather a long story, and just now I have something else to say. No, I'll be honest. To *ask*.'

'What, Peter?'

'It's Fancy.'

'Fancy?' she echoed.

'I was watching you today. Look, I'll be scrupulously honest. I clocked you. You went fine. That horse has pace.'

'No, he hasn't, he – he's just Fancy. If it appeared to you that he had something, it's just that he's very fond of me and I am of him. We simply have rapport, oneness, an understanding.'

'Darling, *you* should be the writer, not me. I love you for that beautiful flow of words, but I still have the evidence of my watch. That horse can go.'

'He has no particular breeding, he was bought out of love.'

'Then for heaven's sake, and mine, race him out of love for me.'

Again she said, 'What do you mean, Peter?'

'It's the third event. An all-comers event, quite open. Nothing very classy will enter, I really mean nothing with experience. They'll be no Cup material, and Fancy could win.'

'I couldn't ... I mean I'm not prepared ...'

'You don't have to be prepared, it's just a picnic race event that always happens. In fact just a "happening" in other words.'

'Nat—' she began.

'Trentham doesn't own him, does he?'

'No, I do, but Mr. Trentham stood the expense of consigning him.'

'As stablemate to the big gelding. Well, Fancy has fulfilled that.'

'I couldn't find a rider at this late hour,' Peta said quickly.

'Here's the programme.' Peter had put it in front of her. 'Gentleman riders. Do you understand what that means? It isn't any snobbery as to who's who and what's what, it's *un*professional riders, so not being able to get a jockey couldn't matter less.'

'Peter, I couldn't ride in a race,' she protested.

'Darling, read again. It's gentleman riders, not gentle ladies.' He picked up her hand and kissed it. 'Me, Peta,' he said.

'No!' she burst out.

'No?'

'I can't allow it. It's only ever Fancy with me and me with Fancy. No one else. Fancy wouldn't understand, he wouldn't react, he only knows me and he only answers to me.'

'Oh, darling, have sense!'

A look must have passed over Peta's face, for at once Peter retracted his words.

'Of course that is the position, and it's touching and beautiful, and I remember how I felt once about a favourite chestnut, but – well, Peta, it has to be, it just has to be.'

'You mean – money again?'

'Not for myself, but – well, for debts.'

'Debts?'

'I've been a fool. I'll have to tell you. The thought of you coming back to me once you left me to fly to England again made me' – a pause – 'unwise.

'I borrowed, Peta. Darling, I wanted so desperately to have things ready for you when you returned that I went much further than I should have, then I found I couldn't pay back. That was when I got out of Sydney. Oh, it was hell, Peta. You were coming to me, but I couldn't wait. And I can't wait anywhere. *Now* do you understand?'

'Peter . . .' she faltered.

'I can't stop anywhere unless you help me now.'

'Peter, it wouldn't be any good, Fancy wouldn't. I know Fancy.'

'I'm an experienced horseman, Peta. You didn't know that, did you? But I am. Why otherwise would I have come up here for a story?'

'Which you haven't got.'

'No. But not because I don't know the game, Peta. I do. But because I have this other thing on my mind. It's there all the time. It never leaves me. I'm frightened, Peta, not of the actual consequences but because . . . well, because it would be the end for me of you. And I couldn't bear that. I'd die.'

'I only ride Fancy myself,' Peta said again, slowly, almost automatically.

'But not tomorrow,' he urged. 'Five hundred dollars. Enough for me to get straight, to wipe off my obligations. After that it will be different. I know it, Peta. I swear it. You can't and you won't stand in my way like this.'

Everything in Peta protested, called no, no.

'I can't,' she attempted. 'I won't. Fancy is – Fancy is different.'

'You've grown different,' he reproached her.

'I waited for you—' she answered piteously. 'I waited in Sydney.'

'I couldn't come because I'd lost every penny in my extravagant plans for my Peta. Yes, I was rash. I'm not a practical man. But I had love, something evidently you had not.'

'I did,' she protested hotly.

'But not when I'm down, is that it?'

'It's not like that, Peter. I'd help you, I'd give you every penny, only I can't give Fancy for someone else's use.'

'I see.' He had let his hands drop away. He had turned away, shoulders drooped.

'Peter,' she called, 'where are you going?'

'Does it matter?'

'Peter!'

He had turned pleading again, reasoning. He had a

smooth tongue and a good turn of phrase, and it had come to Peta that she was being selfish ... that it wouldn't hurt for once ...

'All right.' Her capitulation had been a little weary. Suddenly she was terribly weary. She had been glad when the ball finally had come to a close.

But for all her weariness she had not slept that night. Once she had dozed lightly only to waken in a cold sweat. Fancy. She thought she had cried out, but she couldn't have, for no one commented about nightmares the next morning.

Only Roslyn commented happily on dresses, what, or what not, to choose, and Peta thankfully went along with her in that all-important feminine discussion, for she had no great wish to hurry up that reckoning with Nat. Also she feared that in his inimical way he would find out her decision on Fancy. His brows would raise, his lips go thin. Once, she remembered, he had tossed at her: 'Fancy, of course, is a one-woman horse,' and she had warmly concurred. Yet here she was peddling her horse. Yes, they would be Nat's scornful words. Peddling her horse.

The Blaineys and Peta left around eleven, the girls in the prettiest cottons ... though Peta would have given anything to climb into shirt and jodhpurs and ride right away from the whole thing. For somehow she felt uneasy. A kind of finger on her heart. It was ridiculous. Even though Fancy might not show the speed that Peter anticipated it would still be all right. Fancy was always amiable. He might not be happy with Peter on his back, but he would not resent him. Peter would be quite safe.

—Not once did Peta think: Will Fancy be safe?

Under ordinary conditions, conditions free of emotion and stress, Peta would have goggled at perhaps the most unique gathering in the world. A race meeting with a female attendance that could have held their heads up at Ascot, all the male glamour of caps and silks, but riders as well in crash helmets, leather chaps, and wearing dungarees. Piccaninnies darting between the crowds. Peddlers peddling fairy floss. Shy tents. Hoop-la. A refreshment room with giant urns of tea and great piles of corned beef sandwiches and tomato sauce, scarcely the food for the Ascot dresses, but who cared?

The Downs Cup was to be the first race. – 'While the course it still in fair order,' said Mark Blainey, 'and the crowd more or less under control.'

The horses came out of the saddling paddock and were taken to the barrier, where, being mostly inexperienced, a lot of time was wasted getting them in order. Peta saw Big Kim, who, though unused to such capers as Cups, was behaving quite well. A helper was holding him, but it was not Nat.

Mark called . . . you had to call in such a row . . . 'Your gelding looks good, Peta. I'm backing it.'

He had time to saunter over and saunter back before the Cup began.

'They're racing!' The horses with the medley of riders, silks, crash helmets, greasy overalls spun away.

And right from the beginning Big Kim led the rest.

Well pleased, Mark insisted on more tea, though Peta felt by now that she never wanted to look an urn again in its steamy face.

'You bring good luck,' grinned Mark. 'Any more going?'

'No,' said Peta. Oh, no, she could never give out Fancy as a bet. With every minute she found herself regretting her decision last night. Somehow . . . ridiculous though it might be . . . she felt degraded for Fancy. Fancy had never been called upon to line up to a barrier, to—

Where was Nat? Why didn't he stride over and demand: 'What is this I've heard?' Why didn't he take it on himself to remove Fancy, even though he was not his horse? Why didn't he say that while she was in his employ . . .

'The course is looking a bit battered,' muttered Mark. 'Only takes a couple of races to muck it up. Look how the grass has become worn to dust. I'm glad I'm not on a mount.'

Peta caught her breath. The course did look hazardous. And she had been told that there were always accidents . . . a doctor was needed . . . a nurse.

But still Peta did not think like that of Fancy.

Now the all-comers were lining up, so many of them that even had Nat been present he would have been hard put to have seen Fancy. Peta barely could see him herself. She could see Peter, though, resplendent in borrowed silks. How handsome he was, yet in this moment of strain how little it mattered.

Again, after a long period of settling down, there came that excited: 'They're racing!'

Through a blurred vision now Peta mistily watched the horses, the horsemen low in their saddles. She saw the dust weaving up in patterns, forming a cloud to obliterate the riders.

It happened quite soon after the race began, but not in one of the corners where the racegoers pushed in too eagerly and invited disaster to themselves, but in the open run where there was no danger to onlookers, only to participants.

To a horse galloping down a straight that was not to his liking, that was not the springy grass of Kinrow, or, lately, Garo, but the dust with the crusted earth beneath it of Top Australia. To a horse with an alien rider, a rider with no rapport, with a harsh hand, with—

It was all over in a second . . . half of the horses over in a tumbling mass of hooves and flaying bodies.

Only one horse didn't flay . . . not for long.

When Mark told Peta quietly what had happened to that bottom horse . . . the rider had leapt free . . . she had known from Uncle Claud, from her year at Kinrow, what had to happen next.

'Can I go over first?' she quivered.

'No, Peta, Nat's gone, he'll see to it.'

They took her away, but she still heard the one sharp report and she knew that Fancy was dead.

CHAPTER NINE

THE futility, the utter uselessness that Peta suffered was even worse than her sharp sensation of amputation.

When someone you loved died . . . and she should know

. . . at least you could stand at the window and look up at a sky with a star and feel . . . well, feel *something* that could be understood. But Fancy wasn't someone, he was simply an animal. There could be no listening, seeking, feeling sense with just a horse. Not even with a horse who had been a friend.

Achingly she thought of the new stable waiting back at Garo . . . Fancy's own brushes, Fancy's own rug, own bin, own wooden bucket. She heard Fancy's little whicker whenever she came down to him and she felt a misery so big it seemed to fill eternity.

Everything was lost to her with Fancy . . . the year at Kinrow, Uncle Claud, Aunt Alice, the pollen-golden meadows. England. – Her parents. Lost. Never to come back.

Mark, who had hurried her to the house, comforted her. Roslyn comforted her. The Fiedlers after the race meeting came across to the homestead and comforted her.

Peter didn't come till the next morning, but he was still pale and shaken.

'My God, darling, what can I say?'

His utter wretchedness drove away any anger she might have felt, though anger against Peter had not occurred to her; she, and she alone, was responsible for Fancy's death.

'It wasn't your fault, Peter.'

'My darling, my poor little love!'

'No, Peter, don't touch me. Just go away.'

'I can't,' Peter said bleakly, but Peta had not listened. She had gone to the window again and stared blankly out.

When she had seen Nat come up in the jeep, she had had to hold herself back not to run out to him, but the moment he came into the room she had known there would be no comfort here.

He stood a long while at the door rustling his makings, and then he came deliberately across to Peta, stopping a few yards away. His first words were harsh, unnecessarily harsh, and he knew that himself, but the girl's drained face had shocked him, and gruffness was the only weapon he could find.

'Well,' he asked, 'satisfied?'

'Nat!' she faltered.

'You and you only rode Fancy, your own words, and yet you—'

'And yet I peddled my horse.' She said it for him.

He stared at her an incredulous moment, an incredulity at her admission, and then burst out: 'My God, why did you? Why didn't you come to me?'

'For what?' she asked back.

'If it was money—'

'Would you have given it to me?'

'You know damn well I would.'

'If it was for – Peter?'

'No.' His answer was flat.

'Then how could I have come to you?'

There was a pause, a long pause, and then he said slowly, heavily, 'To sacrifice your old mate . . . no, that's too strong, perhaps . . . to risk him, to risk Fancy, you must have had a very present cause. – You love that fellow?'

'I . . .'

'Answer me, Peta.'

'I don't know. I know I did.'

'Well, I'm not waiting while you go into the pros and cons and come to a decision, because there can be no final answer from you. Not yet.'

'What do you mean?'

'I mean that there is a priority.'

'I still don't understand you.'

'You will. How soon can you be ready to get back to Narganoo? Our crew already have returned to get the plane in shape. I'm presuming you have no more business here?'

'No,' she said, 'no more business.'

'Then twenty minutes?'

'Yes.'

'We can tow the float with us. No need to make two trips.'

'No,' she said numbly, 'not with half the cargo.'

'You're wrong there.' He exhaled. 'There'll only be Big Kim, but there'll be three of us.'

'Three?' she queried.

'My stepbrother as well.'

'Stepbrother?'

'Peter.'

'Peter!' gasped Peta.

'Yes. He is coming, too. He has to. You see, that priority I mentioned is there – in Tasmania. After he settles that business' . . . a shrug . . . 'it's all yours.'

'What's all mine?'

'Your future, Miss Milford. What you do, or don't do, about it. I know none of this is actually to do with me, but by heaven, I wasn't having you overstepping Helen.'

'I can't understand . . .'

'Then that makes two of us. I can't understand either. I believe I never will. Twenty minutes. I'm going back now for the float.'

Peta threw her things in. No need to pack carefully this time, she would be attending no more functions. She went out to wait for Nat's impatient signal, and when it came she turned round and kissed Roslyn silently and pressed Mark's hand. Roslyn was crying openly, and Peta thought: Lucky Ros, I feel I have nothing in me to cry.

She got in the back of the jeep . . . Peter was hunched in the seat beside Nat . . . and they set off down the twisting track through the red ochre sand.

As far as Peta could tell no word was spoken that long empty way. The Fiedlers came out in their landrover to meet them, but Nat refused to go to Narganoo for refreshments. The plane would be ready, he said, and they would push off at once.

At the Bristol, Big Kim was led on without trouble. Peta wondered if the gelding was wondering what had happened. Uncle Claud, who had made a study of horses, had always insisted on their clear memories. Was Big Kim remembering a friendly grey and missing Fancy?

The plane found wings, whirred south, everything that had happened coming up happened again in reverse. Nat went and sat with the crew, but Peter did not take the opportunity to come and talk to Peta. He looked very pinched hunched up like that in his seat. He kept his head averted all the way down.

Peta tried to think, but it was hard and hurtful. She tried to plan, but could find no plans to make. At last she just listened again in memory to Nat saying 'Peter ... my stepbrother' ... and though she still could not fit it all together, she could believe it. That room at Goa ... artily contrived, typically Peter ... that photograph she had picked up ... that swirling text in Helen's house. The drummer and the different music. Peter's work, no doubt. No wonder when she had tossed those lines that first day that Nat and Helen had looked at her, for it was not a well-known quotation.

But where did Helen come in? What was that priority Nat had spoken of? When Helen had told her about Hans and how she was situated because of someone else before Hans, had it been, could it have been—

They stopped briefly again at Alice, and then off again south ... south-*east* this time. When there was blue water beneath them instead of city, mountain or slope, Peta knew they were almost home. The same chequered fields met her eyes again, the sheer lushness after the seared inland almost accosting, almost smiting her with its vivid green, its satin sheen. Everything went off with the same automatic perfection that it had before, but then everything with Nathaniel Trentham would. She wondered a little aridly if he could arrange his heart with the same meticulous results. It would be handy to possess the art of arranging a heart.

There was still no conversation, and Nat, at the wheel again, made no stop for meals. It became apparent later on down the Murchison Highway that they were not taking the minor road into Goa or Garo, but only leaving the main road at the short bypass into the little town where Helen practised. Berribee.

'Lavender House.' It was the first time that Peta had spoken for hours.

'Where else?' It was the first time Nat had spoken ... to anyone but the crew ... for hours. His voice was sharp.

Peter said nothing at all, but very obviously he hung back.

'All out!' Nat had stopped the car now.

'What about Big Kim?' inquired Peta, suddenly as reluctant as Peter.

'He'll be all right for the few minutes I believe this is going to take.'

Nat strode up the path and clanged the door. It was opened fairly promptly by Josef. Peta had forgotten all about the old man, forgotten her doubts regarding him. Now the doubts came flooding back as he stood looking steadily at the three of them, discarding Peta as a familiar figure, discarding Nat, though not so easily, for Nat's rage still showed, concentrating on the stranger. Quietly focusing him ... almost, one could have said, absorbing him. Then with a ghost of a sigh ... or so Peta imagined ... discarding him, too, and saying carefully: 'The doc-tor, yes?' and hurrying down the passage.

Helen came out of the surgery calling, 'Hullo, you pair, I never expected you so soon. I—' She stopped short. 'Peter—!' she breathed.

Peter said bleakly, 'Helen,' and just stood there.

There was a long awkward pause that seemed as if it would grow longer and more awkward.

Nat broke it. He said, 'If this is going to take longer than the few minutes I anticipated, we'd better go inside.' He brushed past the others and led the way into the big kitchen.

Josef was already there, and he must have seen afresh the cold anger on Nat's face, for almost with a little whimper he hurried out of the room.

'Poor old fellow,' said Helen, 'you've frightened him, Nat.' Her voice trailed away as quite obviously her thoughts trailed. 'Why have you come, Peter?' she asked the other man.

Peter looked around uncomfortably, and Peta made a movement as though to leave the room to give the pair privacy. But before she could do so a detaining hand was placed very definitely on her shoulder.

'Not so fast, Miss Milford. Hear what he wants to do. And then, as I told you, you can go on from there.' It was Nat.

As in a dream she heard Peter talking to Helen in much the same strain as he had talked to her up at the Downs. How fate had been against him. How everything he touched had gone wrong.

'Yes, Peter, I'm sure.' Helen's voice came in a little wearily. 'But why have you come now?'

'Because Peta and I . . . because we . . .' With a little show of arrogance, though a rather shabby one, Peter said, 'You must recall, Helen, how I always insisted on clean slates.'

'I can't remember that, but it doesn't matter. You've got one now. I'll put it frankly and briefly. Not only do you mean nothing to me any more, but there's someone else.'

'Then I'm free?' – It was so absurd that Peta caught back a laugh just in time. This man who had only ever imprisoned others talking about freedom for himself!

Helen did not deign to answer, but Nat did.

'Not entirely. Try Peta next.'

Peta turned to Nat in confusion. He looked stonily back at her, until desperately she turned to the other man.

'Peta?' Peter was looking at her in appeal, but not, and she could tell it, in appeal for herself, for her love, but an appeal to help him out of all this. Suddenly clear as to what she must do, what she was going to do, she turned again to Nat.

'Is your offer for Garo still open?'

'Of course.'

'Can I agree now? Can I have an advance?'

If he was surprised he did not show it.

'Yes,' he said calmly, and walked coolly across to the table and took out a cheque book.

'How much advance do you want?'

'Five hundred dollars.'

'That won't take you far.'

She ignored him. She was addressing Peter now. 'It was five hundred you had to have, wasn't it? It was a five-hundred purse for – Fancy?'

'Yes,' Peter mumbled.

Nat wrote silently, tore out the cheque and handed it to her. Peta handed it to the man. For a long moment there was complete silence in the room, then Nat said thickly, as though a rage was slowly choking him up:

'And now get out!'

'How?' Peter had pocketed the cheque and he stood there helplessly.

'There's a bus in fifteen minutes on the Highway up to Burnie. If you leave now you'll have time to walk to the corner.'

'I—'

'I advise you to go.' Nat's voice was even thicker, and looking around quickly, Peter turned without another word and left.

Helen went after him to shut the door again, but that it was not out of sentiment was proven when she came back in her interested and curious, 'Josef is going down the path in a hurry as well. I wonder what he's about?'

Nat did not answer. Peta was quiet. With a little shrug Helen went back to the surgery. Nat took up his things, murmured something about seeing to Kim, said he would be in touch with her regarding the sale of Garo, then went to the door. But, hand on the knob, he turned and looked directly at Peta.

'What you do, or don't do, now,' he said, as he had said before, 'is your affair.'

She heard Big Kim's whicker as he came out of the house again. She heard the truck and float take off. Helen emerged soon afterwards to sit down near to the brown teapot as usual at the big table. Her glance was rueful as she leaned across and filled two cups. 'All right, Peta, shoot,' she invited.

'You mean all the questions I have to ask? I think I can more or less find my own answers, Helen. Except—'

'Except that "someone else" I used to Peter? It's true. I've done a lot of soul-searching these last few days, and it's Hans and Hans only. Though' – a sigh – 'heaven knows why.'

'What do you mean, Helen?'

'Nothing can ever come of it. Our Stas is down in Hobart right now——'

'The special reading?'

'Oh no, that's over. He's meeting his Elisabeta at long last. He's bringing her back here. But' – an unsteady little laugh – 'it still makes no difference to the way I feel about Hansel. I just love him, Peta. Even having him around with someone else would be preferable to being with anyone else and being the only one. So it must be love, mustn't it?'

'What happened between you and Peter, Helen?'

'We met years ago in Sydney, and I believed it was the real thing. I had a course to finish, so it was agreed that I come down later and we marry here in Tasmania. You see my parents had died and I had no one up there. In the meantime to let me study without diversion Peter went on before me to wait. Only' – she shrugged – 'Peter never kept the rendezvous.'

'As he never came for me,' Peta said quietly.

'As he never will come for anyone. That's Peter. After I realized what was never going to happen, I started to pack up again. But Nat stepped in. Nat was wonderful. Apart from feeling responsible he was kindness, lovableness itself. He insisted I stay on, start a practice. I think he must have sensed that I was still uncertain of myself, of my emotions, and wanted me to make quite sure. For he knew that some time or other Peter would come back. He would have to. And as you just saw, Peter did.'

'Only through compulsion.'

'I think it would always have only been through compulsion. If not compulsion from Nat, then certainly compulsion for money, for help.' She paused. 'Am I hurting you, Peta?'

'No. My story could be your story in a way. I don't know what it was with me with Peter, but I do know it's gone now. It might have been the ship, I suppose – moonlight, glamour, something like that. It happens to lots of people. The vision but not the actuality. Nothing true, nothing real.'

'Because there is nothing true or real in Peter.'

'Odd, though,' Peta offered after a moment, 'that Nat is so different. He is the fact, never the fancy.'

'Not odd at all. There's no blood connection. This second wife of Nat's father's brought Peter with her to the marriage. For the rest you must ask Nat.'

'I doubt if I will. Our only communications now will be over Garo. You knew' . . . a little quiver . . . 'about Fancy?'

'Yes.' Helen leaned over and touched her hand. 'And that's why there will be communication.'

'I don't understand you.'

'Well, I'm not telling you. That's for Nat.'

'But our only words now will be—'

'Peta, do you care very much if I don't listen? I've something on my own mind. I'm wondering about Josef. He had a sort of final look about him when I went out and saw him going down the path. Almost as though he was *really* going away. You can't tell by his bag, it's so pitifully little it could just be a bag to take to town for shopping.'

'Does it matter if he does go?' Peta asked a little wearily.

'Yes, oddly, it does. That old man . . .' Helen grew silent.

'Have you looked in the annexe?' suggested Peta, seeing that the doctor was really concerned. 'Does it appear to be empty?' As she said it Peta hoped it wasn't too empty. She was thinking back to those occasions when she had seen Josef moving around the room, fingering things.

'I'll look now.' Helen got up.

Peta followed her down there, and they stood in the small flat. Everything was neat and in order and the same as it always was, but, as Helen had said, there was no bag.

'He's gone, I think. In fact I'm sure of it. But why? And why now?'

'More than that, what with?' Peta knew she said it a little late, and she turned and explained to Helen how she had noticed Josef's absorption in Helen's house.

'I even found him once in Hans's room.'

Helen looked nonplussed, and, turning, she walked across and opened Hans' empty flat. It was in the same orderliness that Josef's room had been. It appeared untouched. About to leave, though, Helen stopped.

'Hans' photograph of his mother. It's gone!'

'Yes,' agreed Peta, 'and it was the photograph that Josef was looking at that time I saw him. Was it valuable? The frame, I mean, the setting, was it—'

'No value at all. I can't understand it. And yet – and yet I think I can ... Peta, we have to get Josef back here.'

'But why?'

'Because I have a feeling that Josef was looking for ... that he was always hoping for ... Oh, it's only a mad idea, but – Look, you wait here and I'll take the car.'

She was gone in an instant, Peta still standing bewildered where she had left her. And Peta was still standing there when Helen came back. Back from the highway.

But there was more than Josef with her, there was a man and woman.

'We were fortunate,' said Hans precisely. 'We get this – this – jump-up—?' He looked inquiringly at Helen.

'Lift,' laughed Helen ... yes, she was laughing, she who had been so preoccupied.

'And it gets us here so quickly. Then Helen is on the highway and she sees us. And here we are.'

Here, indeed, they were. A young man: Hans. An older woman Peta recognized at once from the photograph that Hans had had on his shelf, the one that Helen believed Josef had taken. The photograph of Hans's mother.

But something was wrong with all this. Hans had gone to Hobart to meet his Gretel, as Helen had named Elisabeta, never a silver-haired, middle-aged lady. Peta looked at each in turn, then turned to Helen.

Helen said so unemotionally that Peta knew she had to speak like that to stop singing, 'It's all been so crazy. Elisabeta whom we named Gretel was all the time Hans's mother. There never was a Gretel as I, as we, imagined.'

'But *you* often called her Gretel,' remembered Peta, turning to Hans.

'Because never in my country would I think of calling her Elisabeta. Never in my country would that be right.'

'Then why not Mother?'

'Mama seemed something you did not say here in this new young world, so I did not use it, either. I wished to be of the same – weather?' He looked again at Helen.

'Climate,' she smiled.

'And where does Josef come in?' Peta asked, for without a doubt the old man was well in the picture. He had Hans's mother's arm in his.

'Josef is the first generation in this trinity,' took up Helen, 'and it's a long story, but I think in a way I suspected it all the time. I mean I always felt that Josef fitted in somewhere.'

'My grandpapa' . . . Hans bowed his head respectfully . . . 'after being widowed, travelled out of his country for some years. During those years, bad things happened to us, so instead of returning he tried to bring his children to him. As a result of some of the money he managed to send my mother I was able to leave, and then came his long search for me, for naturally, as he was doing and had done something that could be avenged on my mama, he had always to be very secret. I have no doubt that that was why he left so hurriedly when Mr. Trentham was angry this afternoon, for he tells me that he, indeed, was very stern. Josef would suspect anger against himself. My poor grandpapa has, as you know, few English words. That was why he left.'

'Taking with him,' said Peta, 'his daughter's photograph. But how did he know, Hans, that you were here?'

'There are countrymen who would hear of things and tell him. He would come to see for himself. I think he had been doing that for many weary months.' Hans touched Josef's shoulder with deep affection.

'But it has been worth it,' said Peta, touched. 'For now you are three.'

'Four,' Hans said clearly, emphatically. He looked directly at Helen. 'I have nothing to offer,' his voice rang out, 'not yet, but I feel there will be. My readings this week went very well. I feel certain that I can do much and do it with credit. *I feel I will.* No, I have nothing to offer, but it still will be offered.' A pause. 'Will it be accepted?'

Helen looked just as directly back at him, and then she

stepped forward. As clearly and emphatically as he had said, she said:

'Oh, yes, *oh yes*, my love!'

CHAPTER TEN

'OH, yes, my love.' – All that night Peta lay awake saying the words over and over into the darkness and feeling the tears burning down her cheeks. Never, even after her tragedy, even after the letter from Mr. Gillett telling her about Uncle Claud, in a manner after the loss of Fancy, had she felt so unutterably lonely and empty as she felt now. So lonely and so empty she knew that unless she could conquer it, and how could she conquer it feeling like this, that it must show, and she wanted nothing, nothing at all, to spoil Helen's joy.

One thing stood out clearly, she whispered to the darkness, and that is that there is no place here for me. Neither actually, for in a way there are two families, father and daughter, husband and wife, not emotionally, for I am a friend only. I don't belong. I don't belong to anybody and nothing belongs to me. Even the horses still in quarantine don't belong. I signed them over to Nat Trentham today.

I must see Nat, ask him to hurry the sale. Helen has invited me to stay, to stay, anyway, while she and Hans go to Hobart to find an apartment where later they can be together while she works during the period when Hans gets his degree, but that is only a brief interval, and one that could be bridged just as well without me. One has only to look at Hans's mother to see that even if she has little of our language yet she is still a tower of strength, that she could cope. Also old Josef has not seen his daughter since she was a fairly young woman; it is only natural this little family will not want a third.

Perhaps Nat could advance me another five hundred and I could wait somewhere ... one of the bigger towns ... for the papers to go through. But I must find work. Nat's price is generous, but already five hundred of it has gone to Peter. Why did I give it away like that? And yet if I had it all over again wouldn't I still do the same?

In a way I suppose you could say it was to prove myself to Nat that I did it, though why should I want to prove myself to a man who isn't interested in proof? Though perhaps it was Fancy. I wanted to be vindicated. Perhaps it was . . . She turned her head to the wall and felt the tears afresh.

She knew the sleepless night showed the next day, but knew, too, that no one would notice. They were ecstatically happy, that four. They saw only their own happiness mirrored in each other's smiling eyes. Oh, they included her because they were that sort of people, but they were really not aware of her. Not actually.

'Helen, may I borrow your car?' Peta said desperately at last.

'Of course. As a matter of fact you can forget about returning it today, for today I've referred all my calls to Doctor Jensen. Jenny agreed' – Helen laughed – 'that it was after all rather an occasion.'

'I won't keep it long, I just want to run out to Garo.'

'Darling, run. I've been running since yesterday,' Helen added, hugging Peta, 'In my heart.'

'Keep running,' hugged back Peta.

But once in the car the deflation returned, the longing to be as fulfilled, as replete, as Helen. Coffers filled and overflowing. Oh, lucky Helen!

She turned off down the lane to the old house, stopped the car and walked to the stables, the stables that had been used so briefly, and which never would be used . . . for *her* 'girls and boys', anyway . . . any more. Achingly she crossed to Fancy's corner. Fancy's things still hanging, still waiting, for the grey.

'He's not coming,' she said in a broken little voice.

'That's arguable.' She had not seen Nat in the corner of the stable sitting on the upturned wooden bucket . . . Fancy's bucket . . . but now she did. She watched as he got to his feet, put the bucket right side up in the corner and crossed to her.

183

'I thought you'd come,' he said.

'Naturally.' She knew her voice was stiff with emotion, or at least with the strain of not showing the emotion. 'I had to go through my things.'

'My things now,' he reminded her quite factually.

'Your things,' she conceded.

'Then why come?'

'I wanted to get away from Lavender House,' she burst out a little angrily. 'Everyone is so happy. Did you know about Helen?'

'That she's going to marry Stas, that the third side to the triangle was only Hans's mother after all, that Josef is the grandparent?'

'You did know!'

'Helen jubilantly rang me, though I think I had feelings more or less along this line all the time. But I had to be sure for Helen, she's too grand a person not to be sure herself. That's why I hauled down Peter. He'd let her down, but who knows how a woman's heart works?' He looked obliquely at Peta. 'I don't think she was quite certain herself until she measured him against Stas.'

'Then she *was* sure.' Peta was remembering Helen's shining eyes, and her voice was soft.

He turned a little sharply on her. 'You're perspicacious with others, what about yourself?' At her look of inquiry he said a little roughly, 'Yourself . . . and my stepbrother.'

'You saw what happened, didn't you?'

'I saw you hand over five hundred dollars, but I didn't see you take back a heart.'

'No,' she said slowly, a little wonderingly, 'because he never had it. He was something that happened in moonlight but never something that really mattered. Nat, what are you doing?' For the man was flinging open the stable doors.

'Letting the sunlight in. Seeing things straight. Say all that again, Peta.'

'Something that happened in moonlight but never something that really mattered?'

'No.' Now his voice was quite rough. 'The heart that he never had.'

'If I do say that,' she retorted, 'you'll only jeer at me, at my change of mind.'

'Say it!'

'You'll tell me that it was only because I couldn't bear priority by Helen that I—'

'Say it, damn you!'

'What difference does it make?'

'This difference. *I love you entirely, nothing left out, nothing left behind. All of me.* But I want the same back. Not a heart that's only half there.'

She was listening to him but not believing it. Nat couldn't ... Nat had never ... this wasn't happening to her. She heard herself replying quite coolly, and she wondered how she did it, 'Even if he never had it, my heart I mean, how could you think you could?'

'I don't. But at least I'd start off fair and square. Besides, sometimes I've hoped ... My God, and I've prayed ...'

'You ...'

He nodded soberly. 'I hoped. I prayed.'

'But you were so harsh about Fancy.' She still did not believe him.

'If I hadn't been I would have cried with you.'

'You never said ... you never showed ...' she stammered.

'You weren't in pace with me.'

'If a man doesn't keep pace with his companions,' Peta remembered, 'he hears a different drummer.' She looked across at Nat. 'Tell me about that.'

'My mother died in my earlier schooldays; all I have is a picture of a lovely face. Because I was young, I suppose, my father went into a second marriage. Paula, my step-mother, brought her son Peter. Peter was some eight years younger than I was.

'It was a hideous failure, that marriage. All my mother was, Paula was not. Even a boy of the age I was could see my father growing tired and old. But he would never have done anything, and he didn't, either, when he died. The estate was left strictly between the three of us.'

'Three?' queried Peta.

'Oh, Paula is still around somewhere.' Nat's voice was contemptuous. 'It was not a rich estate. Goa was nothing like it is today, like I've achieved for it. It might have been had my mother been beside Dad, but Paula . . .'

'Your father knew this? Then why did he divide it so strictly?'

'Because he blamed himself as much as anyone else, he had married Paula, taken Peter as his son. It was from Dad we learned about the different drummer . . . he often quoted it . . . he had an obsession for tolerance. No man should look askance at another man, he would always tell us, for stepping to a different tune.

'Paula used to jeer at him. She was an empty woman. She even had Peter make a text of it to taunt him.'

'It's on Helen's wall,' nodded Peta. 'I wondered about the artistic writing.'

'No doubt Peter's gift to Helen. The only thing he could give – he was always broke,' Nat shrugged. 'We were reared on tolerance,' he resumed, 'on the drummer, as it were, so it was only natural that we inherited as we did. I handed over all my money at once in part payment for Goa.'

'To Paula or Peter?'

'To both.'

'Part payment?'

'It was only a third, remember. Then there were lots of extra things to pay,' he said a little wearily. 'It went on and on. Eventually I closed the place and worked. I had to. My God, I worked. For experience I went to the States, and there I worked again. But . . . slowly at first, then quicker . . . I began to get ahead. Not only monetarily but in my experience. I began to know at a glance what to buy and what to discard, do it successfully.'

'You became Mr. Trentham at the studs,' said Peta, 'the man who outbid.'

'Yes,' he said briefly, 'you know the rest.'

'Helen said that Peter used to come back to you, that that was why you kept her down here.'

'That's right. I wanted her to be sure. To look him over again.'

186

'Why did he keep coming?'

'For money, of course.'

'Will he come again?'

'You're his benefactor now,' he reminded her shortly. 'Why did you do it, Peta?'

'I don't know. I asked myself all night. Did I want to – hope to—' Her face crumpled. 'Oh, Nat!' she wept.

'There,' he said gently, 'Fancy's gone. He can't come back.'

'Peter's fault?' She steeled herself to ask that.

'Perhaps . . . he rode competently enough, how couldn't he, coming from Goa? . . . but he was never – well—' A pause. 'No, vindication was not the reason you gave away that money, Peta. What then?'

'To prove to you that I was finished with Peter?' she suggested thoughtfully. 'Though if that was so I was very wrong.'

'Wrong?' he took her up sharply.

'How can you finish something that has never begun?' she said back. Then: 'Oh, Nat!'

For he was holding her as she had never been held, tenderly yet strongly, giving all yet taking all, surrendering but dominating.

'My love.'

Helen had said that and she had yearned over the fulfilment of it. But now *her* coffers were filled.

Beyond the wide-open doors the pansy backdrop of the West Coast mountains rose in velvet peaks and scallops. Nearer still the fields rippled, lush green but promising now that summer was in view, the same pollen-golden of Kinrow. Britain Down Under. That was left, anyway, for her of all that she had lost.

'Darling?' she heard Nat ask of her quiet, and she told him how everything had gone with Fancy.

'Does it matter?' he reproached.

'No, not now.' She put her head against his shoulder. 'Only – only there is a little ache . . .'

'There are always little aches. Though one little one I think . . . in fact I *know* ,. . . I can cure, Peta. Cure by –

another little one.'

'Who, Nat?'

'Brilliant Bess. Was Bess ever so brilliant, darling? Honestly now. Was she your uncle's top class?'

'No,' Peta admitted at once, admitted how it always had puzzled her why Bess had been first in the list to be transported here.

'She was having a foal,' Nat answered for her. 'Your uncle knew.'

'Yes, but—'

'He knew the sire, sweetheart. So what else could he do?'

'The sire?' she questioned.

'Fancy.'

'Fancy? Bess is having Fancy's — But — but how do you know?'

'I became very friendly with Claud Milford, we had long talks. Some of the talks included you . . . in fact I veered them that way, for even then . . .' He tightened his grasp.

'I never saw you until that day you trespassed.'

'I was not trespassing,' he argued as usual. Then he said, 'But I saw you. I saw you dreaming over golden meadows, as your uncle fondly if ruefully told me you did the time that Fancy and Bess—'

'Fancy and Bess—'

'It happens.' His eyes looked darkly warm into hers.

When she did not speak . . . she couldn't in that warm darkness of his glance . . . he said more factually, 'It happens when strappers don't attend.'

'I did.'

'Not all the time.' He ruffled her hair.

'So Uncle consigned the pair of them,' she mumbled, feeling inadequate too late.

'Why not? Wouldn't you?'

'And Bess will have Fancy's foal.' She could see the little wet thing now by Bess's feet, all eyes and wonder and Bess licking it and looking proudly up as though to say, 'See what Fancy and I did!'

So Fancy had not left her after all . . . nor Kinrow, nor Uncle Claud, nor—

'Me, too.' Once again he had read her tumbling thoughts, and, like a little boy, this big man wanted to be included.

Included? But he was all of those thoughts. *All*. Breathlessly she turned and tried to tell him.

Tried . . .

To our devoted Harlequin Readers:
Fill in handy coupon below and send off this page.

Harlequin Romances

TITLES STILL IN PRINT

Harlequin Books, Dept. Z

Simon & Schuster, Inc., 11 West 39th St.
New York, N.Y. 10018

☐ Please send me information about Harlequin Romance Sub-
scribers Club.

   Send me titles checked above. I enclose .50 per copy plus .15
per book for postage and handling.

Name ....

Address ....

City .... State .... Zip ....

MAIL THIS COUPON TODAY